WOLF HOLE

WOLF HOLE

by

Abe Dancer

Dales Large Print Books
Long Preston, North Yorkshire,
BD23 4ND, England.

British Library Cataloguing in Publication Data.

Dancer, Abe
  Wolf hole.

    A catalogue record of this book is
    available from the British Library

    ISBN   978-1-84262-681-8 pbk

First published in Great Britain 2008 by Robert Hale Limited

Cover illustration © Gordon Crabb by arrangement with
Alison Eldred

Published in Large Print 2009 by arrangement with
Robert Hale Ltd.

Dales Large Print is an imprint of Library Magna Books Ltd.

Printed and bound in Great Britain by
T.J. (International) Ltd., Cornwall, PL28 8RW

1

Under a gibbous moon, the old Concord stage swayed and clattered towards the town of Hackberry. The summer had been long and dry, and white alkali dust rose in thick clouds. It stained the sides of the coach and the legs and underbellies of the team of horses, crusted the nostrils of the hard-worn driver.

Some other time, Juce Marble would have taken vital pleasure from the ride, but of right now he wasn't interested. For one night of safe-keeping, he was hell bent on handing over two boxes of gold bullion, then he could cosy into a bed with a whiskey bottle and goose-down pillow for partners. Although there had been no sort of trail trouble for many years, Homer Chupp was inside the coach acting as guard. It was scheduled to be his post until the consignment reached its eventual destination at Bullhead City.

Juce chewed on the ends of his ragged moustache. He was getting weary and his eyes smarted.

'You need the ass of a goddamn grizzly, to slick along this trail,' he shouted hoarsely.

The trail was rising now, approaching a narrow pass in the Vicksburg Cliffs. Once through, Hackberry would lie three miles below and almost in sight. Allowing the horses to make their own way up the slope, Juce stared ahead at the trail, sat with the long reins slack in his hands. He knew every inch of the route, had lost count of the number of times he'd come this way. But now, as always on nearing this spot, his thoughts returned to the events of ten years before.

It was at the top of this gradient where rocky outcrops formed a narrow pass, that the most valuable consignment of bullion ever to be sent down from the mines had been stolen. The bandits had got away with gold valued at nearly a quarter of a million dollars.

No one got wise to the whereabouts or identity of who'd stolen the gold, and a month later a second hold-up had been staged. It was less bullion second time around, but a determined posse hunted down, and, without too much bother or formality, arrested and charged Lew Cayne who'd held a poke of the looted gold in his traps. Within days, the man was convicted of organizing the hold-ups and sentenced to ten years in the Yuma Penitentiary.

Juce harked back those years, mused on the chances of a gold cache somewhere out on the range, somewhere in the surrounding hills.

Lew Cayne was only just out of his teen-age years when he was apprehended. He was well known and well liked in Hackberry, and his arrest came as a shock to the townsfolk. He'd supposedly had others to help him run the hold-ups, had recruited gunmen and brought them to where there were plenty of hole ups and hollows for hiding out. Swearing he was innocent, Lew said he knew nothing about what had happened to the gold, or anything about the identities of the outlaws who'd allegedly assisted him. But that received scant credence when it emerged that one of the guards on duty had actually recognized him. The man had said that Cayne's eyes were so cruel, there probably wasn't any mask brave enough to stay on. But there was other evidence that was more than enough to put Lew Cayne away for ten years. It was presumed by the authorities that the rest of the gang had got away with the loot, either before or after Cayne's arrest. But then, as now, Hackberry folk had talked about the bullion being hidden somewhere in the hills.

Juce Marble's eyes swept the foothills to right and left of the trail. He often imagined that one day he'd come across the gold, and either collect a reward, or go somewhere out of state and trade it in for cash. But with that amount of bullion, neither was likely.

As the coach slowly ascended the rising ground, Juce brought his attention back to his team. The pass was drawing near and, once through, there would be a long and tricky downhill trail to Hackberry when the horses would need expert handling.

Juce put all thoughts of Lew Cayne and gold bullion to one side, started on the words of his favourite song.

I struck the trail in sixty-five,
The herd strung out behind me;
As I jogged along my mind went back
To the girl I left behind me.

'I'd have stayed there with her, if I'd known I was goin' to have to listen to you cater-waulin',' Homer Chupp yelled out at Juce's singing.

The trail bent sharply and, as the coach negotiated the bend, Juce looked ahead and saw a tree lying across the narrowing trail. It was a big, aged spruce, and it completely blocked the route at the mouth of the pass.

He was familiar with the old timber and started cursing under his breath as he drew in the team. It was quiet and calm, but Juce wondered momentarily whether a big summer storm had swept through Hackberry since he'd last passed through *en route* for the mines.

'Get yourself stirred an' out here, Homer,' he shouted, as he hitched the reins to the brake staff.

By the time Homer had climbed from the coach, Juce was standing by the stump of the tree. He was staring down at fresh axe marks that still glistened with sap under the moonlight.

'I knew it was more'n a goddamn gully washer,' he rasped.

Homer was thinking of the gold in the coach. He looked at the broken land ahead, eased his big old Colt in its holster.

'Maybe there's others who want to make quick an' easy money,' Juce muttered. Then he went back to the coach and drew a scattergun from the boot. 'Well, two can lay traps,' he said. 'If that's what's goin' on here, let's set another one.'

The two men made for the cover of a stunt pine that jutted from a rocky outcrop, sat quietly listening to the puff of the uneasy horses. For ten minutes they peered into the gloom, before Juce grew restless. 'If someone was preparin' to hold us up, they'd have arrived by now,' he reasoned.

'Perhaps they have,' Homer responded tellingly. 'I'm thinkin' maybe it's them goddamn Sholto kids. Any no-good deeds within twenty miles o' this place is usually down to one o' their pack.'

'Well, I ain't for stayin' around any longer. Sittin' here waitin' for somethin' to happen's worse than it happenin'. Cover me, will you?' With that, Juce rose from their cover and walked back to the fallen tree. He reckoned that together, they could shift it on its branches enough to get the coach through, and he whistled for Homer to join him.

'If there is someone lyin' in wait, this is the moment they been waitin' for,' he said stoically. 'Reckon I'll shoot me a Sholto skunk, next time I see one.'

'Yeah, well, let's hope it ain't in the next few minutes,' Homer grunted. For a long moment he had another uneasy look around him, then he settled to help lever the body of the tree clear of the road.

2

The two men grabbed at the low, thicker branches, gasped as the deep silence was suddenly shattered by the crack of a gunshot. Homer was hit, and he grabbed at his shoulder where the bullet had taken him. He reeled back, then stopped before crumpling slowly to the ground.

A second shot spat out from a mound of roadside rocks. It was ahead of them and to the right beyond the stunt pine and outside of the pass. Juce crouched among the branches as a bullet whined overhead, whilst Homer lay motionless with blood welling darkly from his wound.

Safe for the moment behind the tree, Juce reached out for his scattergun. He daren't make a break for the rocks behind him, for that would bring him into the moonlit open and under the sights of a trained gun.

'Well, unless they've moved up a grade, I'm rulin' out the Sholto boys,' he rasped. He wasn't going to waste any time or ammunition firing at rocks ahead of him, and the gold wasn't going anywhere, he decided. The horses were anxious. They snorted and stamped the ground nervously, but he knew the brake was set to hold.

He cursed again, when another shot crashed out. But this time he held his scattergun up and over the tree, and loosed off both barrels. He whistled at the noise of the shot pounding the road and rocks ahead of him, thumbed home another two cartridges.

He leaned sideways, wondered how many were ahead of him, *if* they were still ahead of him. Maybe they were already circling. He raised his head alongside a thick, rising branch and took a quick look at the ambushers' rocky buttress. He was in a perilous spot, could be easily outflanked by any number of guns. With his guard partner lying wounded, he'd suddenly become solely responsible, liable, and it bore down heavily. As far as the gold was concerned, he suspected it would be an act of gross negligence, maybe even cowardice if he didn't defend it.

Another shot jolted him from his woolgathering, and then another. Bullets chewed out shards of silvery bark inches from the top of his head. The fallen tree was providing effective cover, but only while he was at ground level. If the assailants climbed higher, they would be sitting ducks. He flung one, quick shot back, but didn't hit anything that counted. Like him, the men along the trail were protected enough.

He pulled one of three remaining cartridges from his pocket, and reloaded. Just one sighting would allow him to take aim, but the hold-up men weren't taking that risk.

It was nearly midnight and there'd be no one along the trail for many hours yet. The men ahead could afford a few hours of waiting. And if they knew that Homer had taken an incapacitating bullet, they'd know that Juce didn't have much of a fighting chance.

With this in mind, Juce was contemplating what to do, when he got warned of being outflanked. Twenty or thirty yards from where the others were still in hiding, some loose stones fell and he caught the shadow of someone edging into more rocky cover.

He raised the scattergun, contemplated levelling out a double-barrelled volley, but changed his mind. It would be a waste, he could be shooting at phantoms, even a big, horned owl.

The midnight air had become hot and clammy and didn't help Juce's predicament. Sweat trickled across his shoulders, between his shoulder blades and down his chest. The gun stock and palms of his hands became sticky. He knew his time was nearly up, that all they had to do was encircle him, take advantage of the fissures and outcrops on either side of the pass. When they were in position, he'd have no cover.

'How do we get out o' this, Homer?' he said in a low, husky voice. 'Drive 'em off by singin' about that girl I left behind?' He thought that maybe he could trust to luck, get across the open ground to better cover at the side of the trail while there was still some degree of darkness. 'But I guess I'll stay,' he half grinned. 'If you ain't dead, someone needs to keep an eye on you ... get you to a doctor.'

Frustrated and angry, Juce elbowed himself up against the fallen tree. He cursed loudly and loosed off one barrel up ahead of him, the second away to his right.

He turned away and slumped back down with his back against the big trunk. Then, off to one side, he heard the crash of a gun, felt the kick, the thumping pain as the flesh of his upper leg exploded.

'Goddamn spoilers got around me after all. Sorry, Homer,' he grated despairingly. For a minute or two, Juce was slumped in a black nothingness, then he dragged his eyes open.

Three men stood over him, their faces covered by neckcloths. One of them stepped forward and kicked his foot.

'I ain't dead, you miserable son-of-a-bitch,' Juce rasped back. He struggled to sit up, but the pain tore through his body and he sank back against the tree.

The man looked away unemotionally, then he jerked his head in the direction of the coach. The others moved off, and after a few calming words, one of them held on to the lead horse's head.

The moon was still high. Its cold light flooded the pass, but gave Juce no further help in identifying any of the three men. He realized he wasn't quite so warm any more, started to shiver as he stared up into the long barrel of the .44 Navy Colt.

Not a word was passed between any of the men as one of them opened the coach door and dragged out two, iron-bound boxes of bullion. The boxes contained small gold bars, all of them bearing the imprint of the Wolf Hole Mine; the very same mine that had contributed most of the gold that Lew Cayne's gang had lifted a decade previous.

The man who'd been tending the stage-coach team, lent a hand, and the two men carried the boxes along the pass to where Juce could now see they'd got a pack horse tethered.

So they'd been well prepared, had known the bullion was being brought through the pass, he deduced. The robbery wasn't a chance trail encounter or mere mischief for a group of Hackberry's idle hands.

The boxes were placed either side of the horse's pack saddle and tied into place. The two men then led the animal to where they'd got their own horses securely tethered nearby.

Juce was gritting his teeth against the crushing pain. He took deep steadying breaths, tried to estimate his chances of making just one reckless move. The man standing guard had turned away to watch as his two partners moved off in the direction of the foothills, had no reason to think that either Juce Marble or Homer Chupp were fit for trouble. And that's what he was thinking, when Juce's right foot sliced through the backs of both his ankles.

The man's legs buckled and he went over faster than felled timber. His gun dropped to the ground as Juce twisted and flung out an arm. The skewer of pain was terrible, but Juce's desperate fingers grasped the frame of the Colt. He rolled on to his back, brought up the gun and wrenched at the trigger.

Again the gunshot split the stillness of the night. But the bullet missed its mark, and Juce knew it. He fired and missed once more, and the man's boot swung viciously into the side of his head.

He clung to consciousness, thought he saw a flicker of movement from Homer as he fought off the seizure of blackness. He grunted and growled, tried to record some detail of the man who'd kicked him. He raised the gun, but the shot came from east of the pass, back from the way they'd come. He tried to grind some sense back into his head, barely heard the second shot as his eyes closed.

3

Leaving the small settlement of Peach Springs behind them, Ansel Agnes, Remigo Correa and Finney Proud, rode under the moon towards Hackberry. They were being employed by Governor Benson Degger to clean up what had been a wild and lawless territory when he'd taken office. The rangers were now five miles back from the pass, pushing on, aiming to reach the town some time around midnight.

Ansel was riding quietly, thinking about what Finney Proud had heard back in Peach Springs. Finney had met an old friend, and from him, had learned that Lew Cayne was back, had been seen in the territory. But the rangers weren't making for Hackberry on that account. The governor had received word that the owner of the Rincon Roost

Hotel, Clarke Mimms, had been identified by a whiskey drummer as the man who, a dozen years before, had been run out of Flagstaff on suspicion of cattle rustling.

Degger had got interested when it was revealed that Mimms had come to Hackberry shortly afterwards. He'd been penniless then, but within three years he'd bought the Rincon Roost and the Sweet Gold Ranch. Maybe the put-about tale that it was inherited money was true, but then again, maybe it wasn't. No matter what, Degger had sent for the rangers to find out about Mimms's current activities. He'd said he wanted the door closed *before* the horse bolted.

Ansel knew it wasn't going to be easy asking questions of local folk without letting on why or what they were investigating. They'd got some reason – chasing the notorious Gemmer gang who'd supposedly ridden south – but it was a bluff with a limit, and presently, Ansel was thinking about Lew Cayne. Finney Proud remembered, like a lot

24

of folk, that the stolen loot had never been found. He'd suggested that maybe Cayne was back to lift what he'd stashed all those years before. But that was nothing more than an intriguing rumour, and if Cayne was back, Ansel wondered if he was intending to restart his hold-up business.

Remigo Correa, the consequence of a one-time Mexican and Apache alliance, rode alongside and glanced at him. Remigo could move as silently as a snake, had an uncanny understanding for the land and its setting. Ansel often thought he could 'bleed' a man of his thoughts and feelings.

'Be a funny thing, if Finney Proud's hunch is right; that Cayne's come back to raise the gold,' Remigo said, as if on cue. Then he broke off, for without warning the silence of the night was broken by the crack of a single rifle shot.

Up ahead of the rangers, the rising trail through the foothills bent sharply west. It was the direction from which the shot had appeared to come.

The three men kicked their horses forward, and within minutes saw the old Concord stage. There were two dark figures lying by a fallen tree. One man was standing above them, two others were advancing with guns in their hands.

Although the range was far too great to be effective, Ansel drew his gun and fired. 'Should break up the good an' the bad, if nothin' else,' he shouted, as Remigo, rode close alongside.

As he'd predicted, Ansel's gunshot had the hold-up men running for cover. Moments later they'd mounted and made a break for it towards the open end of the pass.

'Finney, get down to the coach. Do what you can for them two lyin' there,' Ansel snapped out. 'Use the team to drag that tree out o' the way if you have to. Take the coach on to Hackberry, an' we'll see you there.'

Ansel and Remigo pushed on over rough country after the fleeing coach robbers. They came to the top of a ridge and, under the moon's light, had a view of the darkly shadowed country that stretched ahead. The desolate land was strewn with jagged hills, dried watercourses and stunted scrub.

To the naked eye, nothing moved. Yet under the bright moon, Remigo's keen eyes picked out the distant movement of a lone rider. He held up his hand, used his peripheral vision to try and sight another rider. Ansel held back a few paces, enabled Remigo to head them along the track of an old watercourse that lead down the slope from the ridge. The rider that Remigo had glimpsed was perhaps a mile ahead, but it was a closeable distance.

The rangers' horses were purchased as saddle stock from the fort at Flagstaff. They were responsive and sure footed, and they racked up the pace. At the foot of the slope, the trail zigzagged between low rock formations as it meandered further west.

When they reached the point where Remigo thought he'd placed the rider, the dried-out watercourse forked. With no sound to guide them in the night time's silence,

Remigo slid from the saddle. It was close to where creek water sometimes bubbled to the surface of the dry, alkaline dirt.

The ranger's expert eye examined the softened ground. He saw the hoof marks of one horse that was now headed off almost at right angles to the Hackberry road. 'Goin' north,' he grunted, as he climbed back into the saddle. 'The mount's favourin' its right foreleg. We'll know if we pick 'em up again.'

Ansel nodded, nudged his horse in behind Remigo. He could no doubt follow the trail in daylight, but in the dark, he was a white man; whereas Remigo Correa was half Mescalero Apache.

Ansel thought about the two men who had obviously broken away. They could be anywhere, and away from a yield in the soil, even Remigo might have had trouble tracking them. But he'd be satisfied at snatching whoever it was they were closing in on. They pushed on, and soon found that the track deviated, started to run parallel with the distant Hackberry trail and back in the general direction of the town. The near territory was cracked, hard ground. It afforded little chance of speed, was a good bet that it didn't take the fancy of the pursued rider.

After thirty minutes of hard riding, and with Hackberry lying dead ahead, the luck of the chase went with the rangers. Away to the south, the moon beamed across the lower slopes of the Cordilleras, threw deep purple shadows. Without warning, and less than half a mile distant, a rider suddenly appeared on the crest of a ridge between the rangers and the dark mountains. For a second only, the rider stood silhouetted, but then was gone, plunging down the opposite slope.

Ansel and Remigo spurred their horses off the track. The land was uneven, meshed by treacherous cracks and fissures. Some weren't more than a foot wide, others six or more feet across, and there was no track to follow. Even so, the rangers made as straight as they could for where they'd spotted the rider.

They reached the crest of the ridge, found

that their luck held. The fugitive was now only a quarter of a mile ahead. He was nearing the foot of the slope and pressing his horse hard.

'I'll go,' Ansel said, as he took over the lead. He took his horse down the slope at an almost reckless pace amidst a cascade of dry dirt and stones.

The gap had closed to less than a hundred yards, when the fugitive rounded a towering stack of split rock and twisted scrub pine. Although there was the risk of the man building up another lead, Ansel reined in. He couldn't run the risk of ambush, and Governor Degger was of the opinion that reckless and dead heroes rarely got the job done.

Remigo rode up, and for a few moments the two sat their saddles and listened.

'He ain't movin',' Remigo said quietly. 'He's up there waitin'.'

The rangers dismounted, ground-hitched the horses and moved forward cautiously. Within five minutes, Ansel had a sight of what lay beyond the outcrop. A narrow track cut through great layers of stone that rose high on the left and right, a formation that had cut off the sounds of any continuing run. The moon highlighted the fresh hoofprints that faded into the distance. Their quarry was out in front again, but an unawareness of the land's features deceived the chasing rangers.

Ansel and Remigo went back quickly to their horses and chugged out, rode hard through the chain of gulches and arroyos. They were kicking out of a switchback when the rifle shot blasted out from high on their right. The bullet pulsed fiercely past the side of Ansel's head, brought Remigo up short as it exploded into the ground ahead of him.

Both men flung themselves forward low over the saddle and turned their horses' heads. The mounts came round and reared in fright. Another shot rang out, and the rangers spurred hard back to where the arroyo wall made its sharp bend. They swung down from their saddles, and Ansel returned fire as soon as the rising face of the left-side of the switchback gave protection. He indicated that Remigo should hold in close to the inner wall, while he tried to draw more fire from whoever was ahead.

From where Ansel looked across the elbow of the bend, the stab of flame came from halfway up a deep-shadowed fissure in the rock face. Stunt pine and manzanita had gained a hold, rose as scraggy clumps to a projecting shelf where their adversary had wedged himself. After seeing the way up, the man must have left his horse further ahead before coming back.

'Can you keep him pinned down, while I get above him?' Ansel asked.

'If I can see him, yeah. But he'll have to shoot again,' Remigo answered back, as he levered a shell from the breech of his carbine. 'Truth is, Ansel, I'm thinkin' this might be the time to regroup. We might be just buttin' our noses in, an' I don't think the odds are with us. He was one o' three, remember?' he suggested.

'Yeah, I could easy be thinkin' the same

thing. This ain't really a good night for it,' Ansel said after a moment's thought. 'What do you mean by regroup?'

'Gettin' on to Hackberry.'

Ansel had noticed that the clouds were banking up, the moonlight getting weaker. 'Let's leave him then,' he said and gave a tight grin. 'If we take off quiet, perhaps he'll stay up there for days.'

'Maybe it's that Lew Cayne feller. What do you think o' that?' Remigo said, when they were back on their mounts.

'I think there's work to be done here whether it's him or not,' Ansel replied. 'One thing we do know, an' that's whoever robbed that stage, knows the lie o' the land hereabouts.'

Remigo had learned something of the territory from Finney Proud, and he took up the lead again. The main trail made a great loop between the pass where the robbery had taken place and Hackberry. Remigo reckoned to make straight for town by cutting across the neck of the loop.

They rode for some time in deep darkness, but then the clouds dispersed and the moon reemerged. Remigo had taken them away from the foothills and broken country, had brought them to the rim of a half-million acres of level grazing-grounds. To the south, lay the main trail in its looping detour. Ahead of them, and only a few miles distant, was Hackberry.

The rangers halted for a few moments along the crumbled bank of a dried-out watercourse.

Remigo drew his horse's head up from the caustic soil. 'This gully ain't been washed in months,' he said. 'The dirt ain't even moist.'

The moon's light had grown strong again, and away to their right they could see the low, dark shapes of ranch buildings.

'I reckon that's the place Finney was talkin' about,' Ansel suggested. 'The Kickin' S, an' owned by someone called Buck Scarlett.'

According to Finney Proud, the Kicking S was one of the biggest ranches this side of the main trail. Clarke Mimms's Sweet Gold spread was situated in the better ranching country to the southeast.

4

Avoiding the spiny cholla, Ansel and Remigo set their horses down the bank of the arroyo, and crossed the bed. Remigo reached the top of the opposite bank, and halted in the middle of a thicket of scrub oak. He lifted an arm, slowly beckoned Ansel forward.

The men could see that riding parallel with the watercourse across the grazing ground, was a horseman making for the Kicking S ranch buildings. He cut a slim figure, was hatless, and by the way he rode, they judged him to be a youngster.

Unaware that he was being watched, the boy was within thirty yards of the rangers when he passed them. Ansel and Remigo sat very quiet, moments later watched him draw rein, dismount and lead his cow pony to the corral.

'My pa would've skinned my hide if I'd come ridin' in at this ungodly hour,' Ansel said.

'Mine would've waited. He'd say that what's done in the night, appears in the day.' Remigo countered.

'Maybe we should've stopped him,' Ansel muttered.

'Hah. You really want to stop a kid o' that age if he's been up to no good?' Remigo chuckled. 'I'll go see if those hoofprints bring back any memories.'

Remigo dismounted, left the shelter of the trees and walked forward to examine the ground where the rider had passed by. It wasn't long before he was back shaking his head. 'I don't know who he is, but I can tell you who he *isn't*,' he said.

Remigo meant that it wasn't the rider they'd been pursuing. Ansel shrugged accept-ingly, thought again about what dastardly doings his own pa would have imagined.

Hackberry had a main street, three cross

lanes and a series of inter-connecting alleyways. In the centre, a stand of ash was bordered by mesquite trees to function as the town's square. Beyond the sheriff's office was the annexed courthouse and jail. There was a gallows platform that had once accommodated murderers and horse-thieves. Now it had pink flowering vines climbing up and down its steps.

At the far end of Main Street was the bridge that crossed Trout Creek. There were routes west towards the Colorado River and California, or south to the Gila, Tombstone and Mexico. Between the wagon roads were corrals where horse and cattle sales were made, where range mustangs were sometimes broken in.

The corral was a general meeting place for travellers, men off the trail, and it was where the rangers soon found out that Finney Proud had brought in the stagecoach with its driver and guard. Juce Marble and Homer Tweed were both alive and in the care of Simon Quinnel MD.

In the sheriff's office under a brace of hanging lamps, Finney was with Howard Teach, a ruddy-faced and fleshy law officer who used information and guile to save his feet. Teach looked well pleased to see Benson Degger's rangers, when Finney introduced Ansel and Remigo.

'You find anythin'?' he wanted to know straight off. 'This here friend o' yours has been tellin' me you had someone in your sights.'

'We found him, that's all,' Ansel said. 'But it was *him* had *us* in his sights, most o' the time.' The ranger didn't think he was answerable to the sheriff just yet. He explained briefly what had happened, said nothing about the lame horse, or the youngster at the ranch. Like the sheriff, Ansel knew that information sometimes gave you an edge. Besides, the hold-up men probably had no associations with Hackberry.

Then Teach told them of the gold that had been lifted from the coach. 'Would've been gone by the time you boys arrived,' he said, with a curious, unreadable expression across his face.

'It certainly weren't there when I was fittin' the driver an' his shotgun in,' Finney replied.

Ansel had the strange feeling that Teach had something else on his mind: something along the lines of three rangers turning up when they did, and three hold-up men disappearing.

'It kind o' reminds me o' how Lew Cayne grabbed his loot in the old days,' Teach said, his eyes flicking between the rangers as he flagged up his next thought. 'I'm told he's out o' jail.'

Finney was about to share what he'd heard, when the door-bell pinged and in came a man who, from Governor Degger's description, the rangers knew to be Clarke Mimms. 'He's slack-fitted from his black eyes to the knees of his broadcloth pants,' was how Degger had described him.

Mimms glanced impersonally at the rangers and then looked across at the sheriff.

'What the hell's all the fuss about?' he

demanded. 'What's this tale o' the stage bein' held up at gunpoint?'

'Ain't no tale, Clarke,' Teach responded. 'Juce an' Homer got 'emselves lifted up at the pass. Now they're in Quinnel's sickbay, nursin' their bullet holes.'

Mimms considered spitting on the floor, but he changed his mind and brought out a cigar which he lit thoughtfully. 'What happened?' he said, studiously avoiding the three rangers, and in a manner clearly accustomed to issuing orders.

Ansel managed a tight, wry smile. He'd quickly assessed that Mimms was a dangerous man, and no fool.

As Teach began to explain, Finney touched Ansel's arm and nodded towards the door. Ansel followed him outside, aware that Mimms was watching closely.

'As I said, no gold bullion, but I found *this*,' Finney said, pulling a plated, snub-barrelled Colt from his coat pocket. He turned the butt forward, rubbed his thumb across intertwined carved initials.

'Hmm. Pretty, but it ain't the usual hog-leg a gunny packs, is it?' Ansel remarked, looking closely at the initials. 'You shown it to anyone else?'

Finney shook his head. He handed the Colt to Ansel, and the two of them went back into the sheriff's office.

Remigo Correa nodded at Ansel, a sign that meant there'd been nothing untoward in the exchange between Sheriff Teach and Clarke Mimms. Mimms looked pensive and suspicious, and Ansel had the feeling once again that maybe he was missing something.

By the following night, Ansel Agnes had discovered a great deal about the general set up at Hackberry, and of Clarke Mimms's role in it. There was nothing much to learn about the previous night's hold up, but Finney was certain that his informant at Peach Springs was reliable. But the fact remained that if Lew Cayne was in the area two days before the hold-up, it didn't mean more than he *could* have done it. And it certainly didn't mean he was still around if he had.

On the strength of them supposedly being in Hackberry on the trail of the Gemmer gang, Clarke Mimms had placed at the rangers' disposal a suite of rooms on the first floor of the Rincon Roost Hotel. However, nearly twenty-four hours after the stagecoach robbery, the three men realized that the townsfolk in general weren't interested in rustling. Once it was known that Lew Cayne had been released from the Yuma Penitentiary, practically every man, woman and child in the territory believed he was back. He'd recruited gunmen as he'd done before, and was on the trail again, no question.

5

In one of the hotel's upper front rooms, Ansel sat with his legs stretched out, heels on the window ledge. Remigo stood to one side, looking south along Main Street. Finney lounged on a long, low sofa the far side of the room.

'I'll ride out to the Kickin' S with Remigo,' Ansel said. 'We need to have a word with Buck Scarlett. Finney, you'll be watchin' Mimms's every move.'

Remigo didn't take his eyes off Main Street. 'An' his foreman,' he said quietly. 'He's comin' right now.,

Ansel got up from his chair, took a better look from the window. Big oil lamps were flaring from their sconces, threw brassy light over the sidewalks and into the street.

Morton Frome drew in at the hotel below

them, dismounted and tied his bay mare to the rail beside the wide steps. Frome was big, fifteen, maybe sixteen stone. He had a quick glance at the line of 'punchers' mounts, stepped up to the hotel's double swing doors.

The rangers had learned that Morton Frome had come to town only a matter of weeks after Mimms had first arrived. They'd discovered, too, that the general impression at the time had been that the two men knew each other. When Mimms had bought the hotel, Frome was employed there, and when the ranch was purchased, he became foreman.

'Ain't so odd,' Finney had said. 'When you're that size you can take on just about any job you like.'

'What thoughts you got about Mimms?' Remigo asked, as he and Ansel turned away from the window.

'Well, I don't think he's cottoned on to what we're really here for,' Ansel replied. 'Like most other folk, he's too concerned with the exploits o' Lew Cayne. Whether he's guilty or not, I think Mr Cayne's doin' us a real favour.'

From the sofa, Finney Proud turned his head to look up at Ansel and Remigo. 'An even bigger one if we could tie him in. What do you think?' he asked.

'Maybe. But he would have to be some kind o' numbskull to pull a job while he's still wearin' the Yuma pallor,' Ansel said after a moment.

'There's the gun,' Finney reminded him.

'Sure, and the initials LC. It could be a souvenir from Lake City. You thought o' that?'

'Or Louis Correa. He was my pa,' Remigo added with a grin.

'I'm still thinkin' that Lew Cayne's return to holdin' up stagecoaches is all a bit pat ... a bit opportune,' Ansel said. ''Specially if you wanted the scent of another crime to rub off somewhere else. No. Right now, we got to keep all our options open.'

'An' who the hell leaves their personalized

Colt behind, eh?' Remigo added.

'You'll be keepin' hold of it, then?' Finney suggested.

'Yeah. If it *is* Cayne's, there's no point in lettin' him know we got it. But I'll find out from Degger if it means withholdin' evidence.'

Finney agreed with what Ansel had to say, but he wasn't sure it was *everything*. He had a hunch that something was being held back. 'If Cayne is around, him an' his men will be holed-up in the hills,' he said. 'Why don't we keep our cover by goin' to look for 'em? An' Sheriff Teach is kind of anxious.'

Ansel nodded, 'After we've called in at the Kickin' S,' he decided. 'If what you say's right, Finney – that Buck Scarlett once hired Cayne as a cow-hand – he might know somethin'. An' there's that young rider. I'd like to know what sort o' no good he was up to last night. There was somethin'; I could almost sniff it on him.'

Finney Proud had remembered that about twelve years ago, Buck Scarlett had adopted the five-year-old son of friends who'd died of diphtheria. Scarlett had brought the boy to Hackberry, and he'd lived at the Kicking S, ever since. Josiah Minch was now seventeen, and Finney reasoned it was him that Ansel and Remigo had seen the previous night.

But there was another reason for wanting to talk with Scarlett. At the trial, it was discovered that Lew Cayne knew of the arrangements being made to protect the bullion on its way down from the western mines.

Doctor Simon Quinnel was a long-time Hackberry resident, a friend of Scarlett, and had an interest in one of the Wolf Hole's settlement mines. Knowing of the schedule for transit, it was a certainty that it was *he* who'd talked with Buck Scarlett. It would have been an innocent exchange until Cayne got wind of it.

Remigo adjusted his gunbelt. 'Let's go find out what it was that you sniffed,' he said to Ansel.

Finney Proud knew that Clarke Mimms was

in his private office on the ground floor, and that Morton Frome would, by now, be with him. Alone in the hotel room, Finney wondered if Benson Degger had been completely open with the rangers about their assignment. The Governor was a legislator and politician, knew that retaining power meant not being too generous with anything.

Ansel's thoughts took a similar path as soon as he and Remigo left the hotel. It was curious that, after all these years, a hold-up should coincide with them being hired to investigate the ways and means of Clarke Mimms. There was something else, he knew it, and it ticked away in his mind.

As on the previous night, the rangers rode under a high bright moon. Using the trail that bounded the grazing grounds at the northern end of the loop, they soon came within sight of the Kicking S ranch buildings. Once again they avoided the cholla, set their horses down the bank of the arroyo, and crossed the bed into the oak thicket.

But this time, the buildings weren't so quiet and peaceful. Men were milling in an obvious state of excitement, some pointing, some shouting after four riders who'd set off in quick pursuit of something or somebody. In the light that spread from the open front door of the ranch house, they could see young Josiah Minch and Doc Quinnel. Buck Scarlett was angrily banging the veranda floor with the butt of a Winchester.

'What the hell's happened here?' Ansel rasped.

'Let's go an' ask,' Remigo said calmly. 'We're comin' in the wrong side to be in much danger.'

'I know. But it looks like we've gone an' missed the main event, so let's just look an' learn a bit more.'

Because they were sitting their saddles in silence, Remigo heard the sound of movement away to their right.

'Sure has become a busy of place,' Ansel said, when he heard a horse clipping carefully across loose, dry shale. Remigo held his forefinger to his lips for more quiet.

Whoever it was, was now coming towards them along the bed of the old watercourse. The rangers couldn't move to a more advantageous standpoint, so they crouched low in their saddles, whispered soothings at the horses.

When the rider emerged through the oaks, Ansel moved. He had to, before they were spotted. He held out his Colt, clicked back the hammer. 'It's dark, feller, an' sometimes mistakes get made. So you just keep comin' real slow,' he advised bluntly.

Howard Teach nudged his big buckskin mare forward as the two rangers broke from their tree cover.

'Evenin', Sheriff,' Ansel said, with Remigo moving in close behind him.

6

Sheriff Teach was taken aback and he cursed, jerked back on his mount's reins. 'What the hell?' he started. 'Givin' me a fright. What you doin' here?'

'Hah, I'm sure we'd all like to know what we're *all* doin' here, Sheriff,' Ansel responded, with almost as much surprise. He turned to check with Remigo and they both put their guns away.

'Sorry, Sheriff,' the ranger continued. 'Seems like there's been some trouble out at the ranch. We just seen it, nothin' more.'

As the three men rode on to the Kicking S, Teach explained that he'd been looking around, trying to pick up clues here and there. 'Not everythin's beyond me, you know. Not yet,' he said.

Ansel thought that looking for clues in the

middle of the night, might be.

They arrived at the ranch to find the excitement hadn't died down. The sheriff introduced Ansel and Remigo as Arizona Rangers, but at the moment only acting as interested third parties, not much more than passers-by.

Nevertheless, Buck Scarlett appeared impressed and relieved. Within moments, he'd described how someone had broken into his property and stolen money from his office.

'Cash, I suppose. A lot of it, was there?' Ansel asked.

'Two thousand, cash.'

Remigo whistled though his teeth, uncertain whether that was a lot or not.

'I'm a rich man, Mr Correa, to me it's workin' capital,' Scarlett responded. 'Or *was* workin' capital.'

Doc Quinnel looked up at Ansel and Remigo. 'I heard what happened up at the pass,' he said, with a dry, wise smile. 'Chupp an' Marble probably owe you boys their lives – you comin' along when you did.'

Ansel smiled back. 'Habit of ours, Doc, never bein' too far behind trouble,' he said, winking at the irony.

'I wonder if Lew Cayne knows that?' Quinnel proposed.

'You reckon it was *him*, do you?' Ansel queried.

'Yeah, it's got his mark all over it ... just like down here.'

'Why'd you say that?' Remigo wanted to know.

'Well, who else? He'd know that Buck always has cash around, an' exactly where to find it.'

Ansel held in a sarcastic laugh. 'With respect to Mr Scarlett, Lew Cayne surely ain't the only one to know that,' he suggested.

'Ain't that the truth,' Scarlett gave an agreeable nod. 'Why don't you boys get down from your horses?' he invited. 'See if we can't finish off a bottle o' double-rectified.'

The party were led through a wide door

into Scarlett's private quarters. The puncheon floor was covered in most part with Navajo rugs of bright primitive designs. An elk head hung in an archway that led into his inner sanctum.

Teach looking admiringly at a swing couch that hung by chains from the high open rafters. 'Who was it that saw what happened?' he asked.

'No one,' Scarlett replied. 'Me an' Simon were playin' chess in the back parlour. Josey was upstairs – that's Josiah, my ward, Mr Agnes. There was nowhere locked, an' they must've been real quiet, we never heard a peep.' As Scarlett explained, he lifted an intricately carved cigar box from a desk drawer, showed it around, indicated its emptiness.

'Yeah, the place is big enough,' Ansel said. 'So how'd you know it had happened?'

'I saw 'em. I saw their shadow from my room.' For the first time Josiah Minch spoke up. 'I shouted an' ran down, but they'd got away by then.'

Ansel looked around him. 'Yeah,' he said, appreciating the size of the house, the rooms that ran off. He realized that Scarlett was upset, but he sensed there was more than the financial consideration on his mind. He recalled Finney saying that Scarlett had given Lew Cayne a job. Maybe it was the thought of being robbed by a one-time trusted friend.

'I reckon it could've been some drifter, after whatever he could get. It's the sheriff's job to sort it out, not Arizona Rangers,' Josiah said. 'An' if there's nothin' else to do here, I'll ride into town an' have a look around. You never know, there might be somethin'. You've no objections, have you?' he asked, with a defiant look towards his guardian.

'No, as long as you steer clear o' that goddamn hotel,' Scarlett said. 'You mixin' with Clarke Mimms don't please me.'

Ansel felt Remigo looking at him. He wanted to say that they were staying at the Rincon Roost Hotel, at Mimms's expense, wondered what Buck Scarlett would make of *that*. But there was something else that suddenly interested him – shades of trouble.

'Before you go, kid,' he started, 'if you were up in that room o' yours last night, I'm wonderin' if you heard or saw anythin' around midnight, perhaps a bit later? Whoever it was held up the stage, just might've ridden this way. As I say, I'm just wonderin'.'

'No, nothin',' Josiah replied. 'I must've been asleep.'

To make it look as though he was spreading his interest around, Ansel asked the same of Buck Scarlett.

The man shook his head. 'No, nothin'. 'Cept maybe a lonely ol' timber wolf.'

Ansel nodded like that was all he had to say. But he was thinking quite a bit, like Josiah Minch being selective about when he slept and when he didn't. He was being deceitful, too.

Josiah paused in the doorway. 'Out of interest, why ain't you sure about Cayne holdin' up the coach, or breakin' in here tonight?' he asked Ansel directly.

'Because to my knowledge, the man ain't ever been labelled a half-bake. If *I* was *him,* I'd make darn sure it looked like I wasn't.'

While the youngster was considering a reply, Ansel looked at the incredulous faces, including Remigo Correa's.

'No offence, Mr Agnes, but the whole territory's familiar with the ways o' Lew Cayne,' Doc Quinnel said.

Teach hitched up his gunbelt, added his voice, 'O' course it was him. Breakin' in here's perhaps not quite so cut an' dry, but the stage? Oh yeah.'

'If you don't want me any more, I'll be goin' then.' With that, Josiah gave a troubling look to Buck Scarlett, turned and was gone.

Scarlett stood for a moment with his eyes on the closed door. Then he turned to Ansel. 'I could go along with what you're sayin',' he said. 'It sticks in the craw to believe he'd let me down twice.'

Simon Quinnel stood shaking his head ruefully. 'You're an' old fool, Buck. Never did have the sense you came into the world with. Cayne's taken you for a ride. He *did*, an' it looks like he has done *again*.'

Ansel retained his doubts. He was sure there was something else that worried Scarlett. Something more than the loss of $2,000.

'I ain't on my own in thinkin' what I do,' Scarlett responded to the doc's charge. 'The ranger here reckons as much ... that there's a doubt.'

Ansel tried a thin smile. 'Sounds like you don't think much o' Mimms?' he said.

Scarlett's face hardened with anger. 'Not much, no,' he hacked out. 'The man's corrupt. I think he's usin' Josey to get at me.'

Remigo looked at Ansel and nodded an understanding; that they'd somehow edged closer to the trouble, that it was the Mimms assignment that had originally brought them to Hackberry.

'Corrupt?' Ansel said, with a misleadingly enticing smile. 'There was *me* thinkin' he was a pillar o' Hackberry society. Do you know somethin' that I don't ... that maybe I should?'

Doc Quinnel broke in again. 'Clarke's OK, he won't do the boy any harm. You been listenin' to town gossip for too long, Buck. Ask the sheriff about him, why don't you?'

Teach rubbed his jaw pensively, and Ansel had the impression that the sheriff wasn't feeling too comfortable about something, as well.

'There's nothin' against Clarke Mimms,' Teach said. 'Nothin' more'n you'd expect from someone in his lines o' business. Him an' Buck strike sparks off each other, that's all. Some folk do.'

Ansel knew that Mimms wasn't really a respected public figure – far from it. Yet here were two men that *were,* saying the opposite. He was intrigued that they shouldn't see the absurdity. Ansel recalled how the sheriff had appeared to take orders from Mimms, speculated on just what clues he'd been supposedly out looking for earlier in the night. Before his thoughts got to be manifest, however, there was a sudden outburst of noise from the other side of the door.

Remigo immediately drew his Colt and backed off to the far wall. Ansel moved to one side, when he heard the angry voices.

'What the hell now?' Scarlett barked. He strode crossly to the door, and the others closed in behind him.

Out on the veranda, two boys were being held in the iron grip of one of the Kicking S's wranglers. They were Jack and Bryn, the fifteen-year-old Sholto twins. Both were poorly dressed, had long hair and severe, under-nourished features.

Scarlett cursed. 'I should've known,' he said. 'These pups can sniff out trouble.'

The wrangler said he'd found the twins hanging around back of the bunk-house. 'If they'd come any scrawnier or dirtier, I'd have shot 'em for vermin,' he warned. 'I thought you'd want a word with 'em, boss.'

'We wasn't doin' anythin',' Jack Sholto snorted. 'We was lookin' for firewood. We see one feller kickin' heels away from here,

61

an' your fellers goin' after 'im.'

'Yeah, that's right,' his brother agreed. 'We heard stuff an' wanted to know what was happenin'.'

'An' next year you'll all be invited to the May Ball,' Scarlett mocked. 'So what's your pa doin' tonight?' he added quickly.

'What him an' Ma usually does this time o' the night,' Jack leered. The twins went on trying to pull themselves from the wrangler's grip, their dirt-encrusted faces wizened and screwed up like those of brown bats.

'Cut it out. Let 'em go,' Teach interrupted. 'These kids ain't the ones you're lookin' for, an' we all know it.'

The wrangler hesitated, looked from the sheriff to his boss.

'Take your hands off,' Teach rasped.

Scarlett nodded and the wrangler released his hold on the boys. They scuttled off immediately, ran across the corral and out of sight.

Ansel said nothing, didn't get involved, though he was interested. Teach had acted strangely for a veteran sheriff. He hadn't questioned the Sholtos, in spite of the fact that they had been found hanging about the ranch so soon after the robbery. He seemed more intent on seeing the back of them, having them clear the premises.

Now Ansel had got something else to think about, would probably have a word with the Sholtos as soon as a chance presented itself.

The two rangers stayed on at the ranch for a while. Ansel had one or two questions for Scarlett about Lew Cayne. 'Force o' habit. Never pass up an opportunity to do business,' he'd said, to mitigate any involvement or suspicions that he or Remigo might have.

Not too surprisingly, the Kicking S riders hadn't caught up with the thief, or found any tracks, and the pursuit had been called off. After waiting for the chase party to return, the sheriff wanted chapter and verse, but Ansel and Remigo returned to Hackberry with Simon Quinnel.

The rangers rode alongside the doc's rig

down the main trail and south of the pass towards the town.

'I've been thinkin' about what you said earlier,' Quinnel said, looking up at Ansel. 'Doubts of Cayne not bein' responsible for the hold up. Well, havin' found his gun, what else do you expect, other than a signed receipt?'

'I guess I'll know that when I get it,' Ansel said, a touch frostily.

At the outskirts of the town, Quinnel swung off, saying there was a patient he had to look in on. Immediately the doc's rig faded into the darkness, Remigo turned to Ansel.

'How'd he know about that gun? Did you tell him about it?' he asked.

Ansel smiled tolerantly and shook his head. 'No, of course I didn't. But he knew about it bein' found. I wonder how long it'll be before the penny drops on *that* mistake. There's lots o' curious stuff comin' down at the moment, partner, an' none of it's addin' up.'

'You persistin' with the idea of it not bein'

Cayne or his gang?'

'Oh yeah,' Ansel confirmed. 'An' the more I get to see an' hear, the more certain I am.'

7

It wasn't long after Ansel and Remigo had ridden to Buck Scarlett's ranch that things began to happen at the Rincon Roost. It was from where Finney Proud reckoned Clarke Mimms took the fastest and biggest slice of his considerable income.

At the side of the stairs that led up to the first floor, a door led to Mimms's office. Inside, there was a more private door that led round to the back of the main bar.

At the bottom of the staircase, Finney leaned against the big newel post and watched the swell of the customers. Nobody paid him any notice and he backed towards the door. He knew that Mimms was still in there, and that his ranch foreman, Morton Frome was with him. He moved gradually until he was up close, but as was to be expected, because of its position, the door was unglazed and heavy built.

A drink at the bar seemed a good idea when, suddenly, the office door swung open towards Finney. Into the doorway, a man was backing away from a desk where Mimms was sitting. To one side, Morton Frome sat casually in a high-backed chair.

Mimms looked past the man, raised a hand in greeting when he saw Finney standing there. Hoping that Mimms would think he'd just come down the stairs from the rooms above, Finney quickly took a step forward, but Mimms smiled, beckoned him forward.

The man was Wallace Egham, owner of Hackberry's lumber yard, and Mimms quickly told him that their account was settled, and to let him have a bill of sale.

The man turned and looked at Finney, then back at Mimms. 'Yeah. Yeah, I'll do that,' he said with a slight falter. 'You didn't mind me callin' in, then?'

'No, o' course I didn't,' Mimms returned. 'I overlooked it, 'cause of all the other stuff that's been goin' on.' Then he got to his feet and called out to Finney. 'Step in, Ranger,' he said, as Egham edged past Finney on his way to the saloon's front doors.

Finney shook his head. 'Thanks, but I was just passin',' he said cheerily. 'Just got taken aback there for a moment, by the size o' this evenin's congregation.'

The ranger took his time in making his way to the bar. He was thinking about the happenings in Mimms's office. He had a hunch that whatever it was, it wasn't about Mimms shelling out for some new floor-boards. What's more, he had something on Wallace Egham. Apparently, the man hadn't always been the proprietor of the lumber yard. It seemed that ten years ago – a fairly seminal point in the annals of Hackberry – Egham had been employed by the Wolf Hole Mine, had ridden as guard when Lew Cayne had lifted the last consignment of bullion. In fact, he'd been the one who'd sworn he'd seen Cayne with his mask off. It was his evidence that had been conclusive at the trial. Finney was of the opinion that if Lew Cayne was free of Yuma Penitentiary, Egham was a man who ought to be treading real careful. What the hell he was now doing with Mimms, went through Finney's mind, as he stepped up to the bar to order himself a beer from a surly barman.

'I'd like you to pour me an under-measure o' warm froth in a grimy glass,' he said.

The barman looked hard at Finney, thought for a moment, 'Not in here,' he flung back with a disagreeable smile.

Finney gave the man an unreadable look. 'Good. I'll put the last time down as a fig-ment o' my imagination,' he said.

Finney had been at the bar no more than twenty minutes, when someone else he recognized came into the saloon. It was the swagger, age and smarter-than-average range clothes that the youngster wore that tagged him as Josiah Minch, the ward of Buck Scarlett.

Finney faced the bar, eyed the youngster through the mirror, watched as he went straight on through the saloon to Mimms's office door. The man gets more visitors than a neighbourly wagon cook, Finney mused.

Minch had been with Mimms for a good half-hour, he estimated, when the front swing doors opened and a man walked through unhurriedly. He was a man who was middle-cut in terms of height, build and age. Two striking features were the intensity of his grey eyes and the low-slung Navy Colt.

'Ain't much mistakin' you, feller,' Finney muttered as Lew Cayne stepped into the saloon.

'Hell's bells, it's Lew Cayne,' someone who was standing close, said aloud.

As an awed, fearful silence spread, Finney immediately thought that now was the time to have his quiet drink. That was followed by the wry question of whether Cayne had come to visit Clarke Mimms in his office.

'Huh, I was told that absence makes the heart grow fonder,' Cayne said, his words cutting through the charged silence. 'Well, I guess they could've got that wrong. Ain't

none o' you pleased to see me? No one goin'
to buy me a drink for ol' times' sake?'

Finney was about to say he'd stand him a
drink, for nothing more than entertainment
value, but he didn't have time, because
Mimms suddenly appeared with Morton
Frome.

'I wondered what the sudden hush was
about,' Mimms said, the surprise making
him almost too quiet to be heard.

The two men stared hard at each other,
but then Cayne switched his attention to
Frome.

'I guess you ain't too pleased to see me,
eh, Mort?' he said, the challenge resonating
clear.

Frome moved forward, pushed away the
restraining hand that Mimms had laid on his
arm. He elbowed his way through the group
and closed up on Cayne. Finney pushed his
empty glass across the bar and went after
him. He'd seen the hostility set across
Frome's face, recognized the impending
danger for most everyone in the saloon.

As he went after Frome, he saw out of the corner of his eye that Mimms was coming too. But Finney hadn't the time to pay them much attention. He acted so quickly, that nobody in the saloon saw his hand draw his Colt and slam the long barrel into Frome's great bony wrist.

Frome still managed to pull his own Colt, but on clearing the holster the man grimaced at the sudden bite of pain. He dropped the gun and it crashed loudly to the sanded floor. He cursed and swung round, found himself facing Finney's own Colt that was now pointing at his chest.

'Sorry about that. But in the absence o' Mr Teach, I'm the next best thing you got to a lawman, an' this hotel ain't the best or safest place for any wild shootin',' Finney stated coolly.

Frome's lips drew back and tightened over stained teeth, and his eyes glowered. 'There's two fellers laid up' in Doc Quinnel's right now could tell you a thing about wild shootin',' he snarled. 'You forgettin' what happened up at the pass? I got a right to make goddamn sure Cayne gets what's comin' to him.'

Finney shook his head decisively. 'While we're standin' here like this, you got no rights that I can see.'

Cayne remained motionless, watching, making no move for any sort of retaliation. The saloon's customers stood quiet, tense, except for Mimms who picked up Frome's Colt and moved up beside Finney.

'Thanks, Ranger,' he said. 'An' there was me thinkin' I was the safeguard o' my own property.'

Lew Cayne showed no emotion, even when he spoke up. 'So, the story's goin' round that it was me held up the coach?' he levelled out. 'I'd heard about it, o' course, but didn't really believe it. I didn't believe that anyone in Hackberry could be so goddamn bone-head gullible an' pig-wit stupid. So, I'd say it's got to be somethin' that you thought up, Mort,' he said, looking from Finney to Mimms, then Frome.

Frome grunted and, disregarding the threat of Finney's Colt, he swung round, lunged his ham fist up and across Cayne's jaw. It wasn't a practised or accurate blow, but Frome had a lot of his big body behind it and Cayne was unprepared.

Cayne reeled, staggered and fell backwards heavily. He pushed a hand towards his smashed mouth, and for a few moments it looked as though he was down and out.

Uproar broke out instantly in the saloon. The cowhands grabbed their glasses tighter and surged forward. They pushed Finney aside as though his order of restraint had been lifted, and surrounded the two combatants.

Cayne struggled to his feet. His mouth and chin were running with blood, but his eyes were bright.

That's the pen for you, Finney thought. You don't come out o' there, heifer branded.

Morton Frome lowered his big head. He rubbed his wrist, wondered what was coming now as the inevitable strike back.

The cowhands took a pace back in anticipation. This wasn't the first fight the saloon had witnessed. When things got dull, and a man's temper coincided with a bellyful of whiskey and beer, there'd be a regular bout of rough and ready fisticuffs.

Finney wasn't going to intervene now. Guns were one thing, fists were another. And the cowhands had scented blood, weren't likely to put up with any out-of-town interference. To Mimms's way of business thinking, they were customers and always right.

Cayne rolled onto his knees, came to his feet and circled to his right. Frome went forward and Cayne stepped further to his right. He was conscious of the men ringed around them, and for a brief moment appreciated the wild absurdity of this. Then he saw Frome wheel, halt and squint against the lights along the mirror of the back bar.

He quickly came at Frome, and with every ounce of his weight behind his right arm, he drove his fist low into Frome's side. With the knuckles of his left hand, he slammed into the side of Frome's head. The two blows were almost simultaneous. Frome gave an intense grunt as the double pain hit him. He stepped back, fought for breath, as Cayne swarmed at him.

Cayne moved himself front on to Frome, unmercifully drove at the man's vast midriff. Then he lifted his fists to the heavy face. Frome tried to set his ground, but Cayne was now chopping at the muscles in his arms, pummelling his face.

With strange, perverse fascination, Finney stood watching. With the run of blood from Frome's nose, he realized that Cayne wasn't trying to finish off the big man. He's punishing him, he thought. Finding something to savour with every blow.

Frome covered his face with his arms, and went straight at Cayne as if to tackle him. Cayne took a quick, half-step back and brought his knee up. But Frome's momentum carried him on, his massive arms wrapped around Cayne's legs.

Again, Cayne went down, landing with a bone jarring crash on the puncheoned floor. But the falling had broken Frome's grasp and Cayne managed to raise a knee into Frome's face. He heard Frome groan, dragged a leg free and kicked savagely at the man's head. Frome rolled away, spluttering and cursing wildly.

Cayne came up in a crouch, was only then aware that someone was holding his arms. He fought to free himself, drew in a long gasp of stale, smoky air as he was dragged to his feet.

'I ain't ever been much of a bludgeon-man, but I reckon I've waited nearly ten years for that sort o' welcome,' he wheezed through swollen lips. Then he shook himself free of the two men who were holding him and spat disgustedly down into the dirty sawdust. He nodded at Finney, but without even glancing at Clarke Mimms, he wiped his mouth with the back of his hand and pushed his way back and out through the saloon doors.

Finney looked down at Frome who was also being watched impassively by Mimms and Minch.

'That's it, next one's on the house,' Mimms called out. 'A couple o' you help Frome, an' someone knock a tune out o' that goddamn pianner.'

Finney wasn't in the mood for another beer, so he sat on a bench outside of the hotel. He looked up and down the main street, but knew there'd be little sign of Lew Cayne. For a while he thought about how he'd recount such a stirring yarn to Ansel and Remigo, wondered how long it would be before their return.

8

The fight was fifteen minutes over, but the large single-roomed saloon was even more crowded now. Word had got around the town that Morton Frome had been floored, and folk had arrived to hear the story of Lew Cayne's dramatic appearance, his bloody and thrilling fight with Clarke Mimms's mighty foreman.

'Yessir, he sure must've had someone or some-thin' on his side,' one of the old wiseacres was saying, over and over again.

Having seen Cayne slip away, Josey had then watched as Frome was helped back to Mimms's office. After a few more minutes, the crowd got around to wondering where Cayne was, but by then it was too late. Another of the saloon's customers had wondered what Cayne had meant about Frome not being too pleased to see him.

'There's more to *that* than meets the eye,' he'd said, but wasn't aiming on bringing the foreman to account.

Later, Cob Sholto snaked into the saloon. Jack and Bryn's father, a tall, angular and unkempt figure, was the sort of man who skirted eye contact, mostly trod a solitary path. He made his way through the ebbing excitement towards the end of the bar. Josey saw him and, after a moment's hesitation, he slipped unnoticed through the bar's exit into the alleyway at the rear of the hotel.

Josey cursed as he avoided the boxes, bags and bins of refuse. 'An' these must be the offices o' Cob Sholto,' he muttered with amused disgust. He edged along the wall keeping tight within deep shadow. It was a warm, breathless night, and he'd seen Mimms draw up his office window when they'd brought the near unconscious Frome in. It was still open.

Josey could clearly hear the voices and what was being said, knew he couldn't have missed much.

'So, you goin' to tell us what it is you got?' Mimms was asking.

'Information's a commodity,' Cob Sholto replied. 'It's important to know its value.'

'I do. Just *you* don't set it too high,' Mimms advised.

'You want to know where Cayne is?'

'Yeah. An' if you don't tell me real soon, I'll set my foreman on you. He's damaged a bit, but he'll snap your wings easy enough, Sholto.'

There was a pause, and Josey heard Mirnms say something about that being *it*. He guessed that Mimms handed over some sort of payment, then Sholto spoke up.

'He's usin' an empty rock miner's shack. Leastways he *was* this afternoon. He's got some trappin's there, so it could be he's holin' up. It sort o' makes him a neighbour o' mine. An' maybe us Sholtos ain't that far from a golden cabbage patch, eh, Mr Mimms?'

Josey could hear the sly suggestion in

Sholto's voice. He wished he could see the man's expression, but daren't move to take a look.

Mimms started to say something back, but Josey heard footsteps from the other end of the alley. He cursed, spun away from the rear wall of the hotel and ran for the front corner of the building. He turned out of the alley before whoever it was could have seen him, then made a short leap for the steps that led to the hotel's front swing doors.

Josey leaned against the wall just inside of the saloon, took a few relieved breaths and ran a couple of thoughts through his head. Cob Sholto knew where Cayne was, because he'd seen him there. Josey knew, because he'd just overheard Sholto saying so. But Clarke Mimms had paid for the information. Josey knew Mimms reasonably well, and had a pretty good idea why. He also reckoned he knew what the man would do now.

Josey had just worked out what his own next move must be, when he noticed

Wallace Egham move from behind the bar into the saloon proper. Josey swore to himself, thinking that the man must have come in from the door that led to the alley-way. He cursed again when the man looked up and nodded, started to make his way over. Josey didn't like the lumber-yard owner, never had, not since he'd wanted five cents for a sack of sawdust that Josey had wanted for the floor of his rabbit coop. And that was seven or eight years ago.

If Egham had come straight from his yard, Josey estimated that he could have used the alleyway. If so, maybe he *had* been seen listening at Mimms's window. Josey put it down as another reason not to like him.

'Evenin', Mr Egham,' Josey got in quick as Egham approached. 'You're workin' kind o' late.'

'That's what lamps were invented for, son,' Egham responded smartly. 'An' you? You here waitin' for a game?' he said, with a voice that reminded Josey of one of his rip saws.

'Yeah. I guess there'll be one when Mr Mimms gets through. I need to get back some o' my losses.'

Egham didn't reply, but a thin smile played across his otherwise blank face. Josey hoped that it meant he didn't think much of his chances of winning anything back. He didn't really know where Egham had been during the fight. The man hadn't given anything away, just the unreadable smirk.

Before he could say anything else, Josey saw that Clarke Mimms was signalling for Egham to join him, just as Cob Sholto was exiting Mimms's office by the rear door.

'Game tonight, Mr Mimms?' Josey called out hopefully. 'Later on maybe?'

Mimms thought for a moment, struck a quizzical expression, then shook his head.

Josey accepted the negative response, shrugged and turned away. So that's it, he thought, no game, not even the time o' day for *me*. But there's certainly something in this night for Wallace Egham.

Josey rode from Hackberry towards the

Kicking S. For anyone following, that's how it looked. But when he came to the point in the trail where he would normally turn off to the ranch, he drew rein and dismounted. He climbed the rocks and set himself up to watch the trail he'd just covered. Under the bright moon, he waited quietly for ten minutes, until he was satisfied there was no one following him. He scrambled down from the rocks and remounted, but for the second time, it wasn't in the direction of the Kicking S. He rode northwest, steadily through rougher country towards the shadowy foothills of the Cordilleras. He'd get to where he was going long before striking the first, low crumpled ridge of the mountains.

'You just got to be out here somewhere,' he muttered, straining his eyes and ears.

Fifteen minutes later he dismounted again, looped his reins around the branch of a dried-out mesquite. He was at the lip of an arroyo that dropped thirty feet, but from where he stood, was only a few feet across.

Except for a few hundred yards where it

surfaced to look up at a narrow band of sky, the dried-out bed was a sometime break in the land for Song Creek. The water course ran underground until it surfaced further west *en route* to Bullhead City. Along the creek bed, there was a string of cutback caverns, where the watercourse had once scoured the sedimentary rock. It was where, as a kid, Josey had often holed-up with his Hackberry school friends, spent hours fighting off imaginary Apaches.

Cautiously, Josey wedged a foot into a fissure, leaned out and looked down into the darkness of the now, bone-dry creek. For a minute he listened to the weird sighing notes of the night breezes that played across the mouths of the caverns and up along top of the arroyo.

It was when a build up of dark cloud drifted in front of the moon and his pony snorted, that he had the first inkling of something being wrong. He cursed, dragged his foot from the narrow cleft, but it was too late.

The man jumped at Josey's back, dragged him back a few feet, then twisted him to the ground. Josey tried to grab his Colt, but the man kicked out at his wrist. The man was big and heavy and Josey felt rough, hard fingers encircle his throat. In the darkness he writhed and twisted, as the blood pounded in his temples. As he turned over he desperately kneed up, then again, and a third time, before the iron hands relaxed. Josey kicked himself away and struggled back to his feet, but the big man was on him again. A fist caught Josey in the chest and he staggered backwards, felt the mesquite trunk slam between his shoulder blades. His pony snorted in alarm, dragged back on its hitch. Josey took a faltering step forward, then sideways as the man closed in again. Josey tripped, went on, as the man took a lunge at his legs. He fell, hit his head and realized he was halfway over the edge of the arroyo. He rolled sideways but the man took a kick and Josey doubled up this time, his weight shifting, taking him full over the edge. His legs thrashed as he sought to swing them up and crawl back over the edge, but the man stamped on him. As he went down in to the deep darkness, his fingers gripped forlornly at the shale and dirt that slid away beneath his body and he gasped with the effort of trying to stop his fall.

Halfway down, Josey struck the bulging, exposed roots of the mesquite. He made a futile grab before rolling out and down again. But the windings of gnarled wood were enough to break the impetus of his fall, striking his body and knocking him around. Josey hit the floor of the arroyo almost standing. His knees went with the sudden impact, but he knew he wasn't dropping any further as he slumped into oblivion.

The man who'd jumped him appeared as a black silhouette against the dark sky. As if on cue, the moon reappeared, the sky lightened and he could see Josey lying motionless thirty feet below. Wanting to make certain he was dead, the man drew his gun and took a two-handed aim. He held still for a moment, looked around him and listened.

Further up the slope of the hill, west of the gorge, he thought he caught the movement of a shadowy figure. He thought better of putting a bullet down into Josey's body and cursed.

9

Not far from the pass on the main trail where the stagecoach had been held up, the three rangers dismounted and led their horses off the trail. Having heard Finney Proud's account of what had happened at the hotel while he'd been out at the Kicking S ranch with Remigo Correa, Ansel Agnes decided to look for the shack where Cob Sholto had seen Lew Cayne.

They weren't far from the Sholto house when Ansel called a brief halt. The three of them sat their saddles and exchanged information. Ansel told Finney of the break-in at the Kicking S.

'Well, it couldn't have been Cayne then,' Finney observed. 'Not unless he sprouted wings, an' made it to town in ten minutes.'

It was late enough for them to assume that

Cayne would be back at the shack. Making time wasn't that important, unless the man was undertaking more night work. A hundred yards off the trail, the rangers crossed a thicket of trail scrub and low mesquite, and they hauled in again.

As Finney knew little of the events at the ranch, Ansel recounted what had happened since he and Remigo had left Finney at the hotel. He told of the stealing of Scarlett's cash, the subsequent and abortive pursuit of the thief, and conversations with Scarlett, Doc Quinnel and the sheriff. He described Scarlett's passage of arms with young Josiah Minch, and of the tussle with the young Sholto twins. 'Scarlett was talkin' of years gone by, an' I got the distinct impression he still holds a sneaky regard for Lew Cayne,' he said.

'Couple more things,' Remigo added. 'The feller who broke into Scarlett's office, is the one whose mount favours its right foreleg.'

'What's the second,' Finney said after a moment.

'The good doctor, Simon Quinnel, slippin' up when he mentioned the gun from the coach.'

'Oh yeah,' Finney said. 'Reckonin' one of us had talked. That's a *real* mistake if ever there was one.'

Remigo stared thoughtfully across the rough land where the moonlight still threw its pale light. If Simon Quinnel had known about the gun being left in the coach, he'd assumed that Sheriff Teach would have been informed. The point was, how had he known?

'You must have known about young Josey comin' into town?' Finney asked of Ansel and Remigo.

'Yeah, we knew,' Remigo said. 'An' he had a cute way o' lettin' his guardian know.'

'What do you make o' Wallace Egham payin' Clarke Mimms a visit? He ain't exactly cut from the same chaw.'

Ansel shook his head. 'Don't know. It's interestin' though ... ain't likely to be somethin' above board,' he said. 'An' you say it was him that saw Lew Cayne on the trail all them years ago?'

'Yeah. I bet he's wishin' he kept his mouth shut. He must be quakin' in his boots.'

'Hmm, well, maybe that's what figures. There's other stuff too,' Ansel rumbled. 'Like Teach's funny treatment o' the Sholto kids. It was almost kindly, uncle like. An' what the hell was he really doin' there at that time o' night? An' why does he seem to reckon it ain't got anythin' to do with Cayne?'

'Hey, Finney. If you was usin' ranger muscle at the saloon, how come you didn't arrest Lew Cayne,' Remigo asked.

'No proof an' no evidence. Nothin' to implicate him even. Can't arrest a man just 'cause a coach gets held up. Everyone's got to be somewhere. Even Governor Degger might raise an eyebrow at that sort of evidence.'

'It weren't *him,* boys,' Ansel contributed. 'I just know it. But someone's tryin' real hard to finger him ... make it look like it. I mean, when was the last time either o' you left your gun behind?'

Remigo smiled. 'Yeah. Now we got to start

wonderin' what it was them Sholtos saw at the ranch. It might explain why the sheriff was so keen to get 'em safely packed off.'

'It could be,' Finney agreed. 'An' what was Lew Cayne doin' wanderin' into town, if he's in the middle of a goddamn hold-up tour?'

'There's lies an' half lies here – truths an' untruths, an' we been hearin' 'em for some time,' Ansel said.

'Josiah Minch must've known Lew Cayne,' Remigo suggested. 'No more'n fry size, but he would've known him.'

'What do you mean by that?' Ansel asked.

'Don't know, just sayin'. We been lookin' to the left, while somethin's been slippin' by on the right. Maybe we got to start takin' notice o' the sidelong stuff.'

Heavy cloud was now banking up in the sky, and now and again the moon disappeared from view. But the rangers stayed safely put.

As they organized thoughts and considered proceedings, Remigo suddenly held up his hand for silence. He'd picked up a sound that he knew wasn't natural or made by a night critter. He indicated their guns, quietly drew his own Colt and then, without a word, he was gone. He darted silently between low rock and scrub formations, made towards the trail fifty yards away. Ansel and Finney accepted it was a job for his talents.

A long minute passed, and then Ansel and Finney heard Remigo shout for them to follow.

'Just stay where you are, don't even waggle your tongues,' they could hear the ranger threatening as they ran up.

'Christ, don't these Sholtos ever go to bed?' Ansel snapped, when he saw who Remigo had got covered. 'They really are life o' the desert.'

'We was runnin' for help. He's dyin' or dead, down at the creek,' Jack Sholto gasped.

'Calm down, no one's goin' to harm you,' Ansel said as calmly as he could. 'Who's dyin'?'

'Josey Minch. He's down in the arroyo

bed. He ain't movin'. I reckon he's dead, mister.'

'Did you see anyone else there?'

'Yeah, don't know who though. It was real dark. He saw us, but we lost him in the scrub.'

Remigo grinned. 'Somethin' you boys must be real good at,' he said appreciatively.

'You got to come. Maybe he'll come back,' Jack pleaded.

'Can you take us there?' Remigo asked.

Bryn Sholto nodded. 'We can run you,' he said, intrepidly.

On the return to Song Creek, the boys only let up their running once or twice. That was to wait for the rangers in their ride through the thick, thorny scrub. As they neared the arroyo, Jack stopped to talk to Ansel.

'We gettin' dollars for this?' he asked, appearing to stand his ground.

'I hadn't thought about that yet. But, yeah, I guess so,' Ansel said. 'An' there's one or two *other* things I want to discuss with you, kid. Now get goin'.'

They reached the arroyo, but only after Remigo had dismounted and gone ahead to scout. But the area was deserted, and Ansel and Finney came on with the twins. They had a look over the rim of the arroyo, knew that the twins had got it right. In the dark below, they could see Josiah Minch and unmistakable movement.

'I reckon you saved his life, boys,' Finney called out.

'Hopefully earned 'emselves that reward,' Ansel replied, as he tied a rope around his waist. 'Comin' to get you, Josey,' he then shouted.

On the bed of the waterless arroyo, Josey had dragged himself to his knees. His head was aching, and for the moment his limbs were unwilling to obey him. But he was young and tough, not seriously injured. It was the tangle of mesquite root that had broken his fall, probably saved him from fatal injury.

Loosening the rope, Ansel was soon beside him to help him to his feet. 'No need to thank me just yet,' the ranger said cheerfully, 'just wait till we get up top.' Ansel then looped the rope under the boy's shoulders and called out for Finney and Remigo to haul him up.

Ansel took a step backwards to watch Josey make his way steadily upwards. His foot twisted on a piece of rock and he looked down, went to flick away the offending obstacle. Then he picked up the small bar of gold that glinted in the moonlight.

'This weren't left by no gully wash,' he muttered with astonishment. The bar was stamped with three linked triangles that formed the imprint of the Wolf Head Mine.

'I got a keepsake, somethin' else for us to think about,' Ansel said when, a few minutes later, he rolled on to firm ground above the arroyo.

10

Ten minutes, a few gulps of water and Josiah Minch was better recovered. He was badly bruised from the fall, and his neck was hurting where his assailant's hands had squeezed but there were no broken bones. He'd fainted on hitting the arroyo bed, then recovered only to lapse into woolly darkness again. When the rangers arrived, he'd heard their shouts from above, found a motive for staying conscious.

The Sholto twins had gone by the time Josey was talking. Ansel had questioned them, but found out little more than he already knew. He warned them of the dangers of flapping their mouths about what had happened. 'I'll be round to see you boys tomorrow,' he promised, his voice heavy with inference.

'Now for your story, kid,' Ansel said, watching Josey rub life back into his arms and legs. 'What the hell were you doin' up here gettin' yourself beat up so?'

Josey shook his head because he had no idea who'd attacked him. He'd only seen and felt a big dark shape. There was no way he could tag on a name.

Ansel noticed that Josey avoided the first part of his question, and before he could ask again, the youngster's talk was of leaving.

'I've got to get moving,' he muttered. 'Thanks for bringin' me up, mister. I'm grateful, but right now, I've got to get–'

'Movin', yeah, you just said,' Ansel interrupted. 'I understand that.'

Josey was anxious about something and it showed. He set his jaw, and his eyes darted from side to side as though searching for a way of escape.

'Look,' Ansel continued. 'We get tipped off you're in trouble, an' we ride here to get you out of it. Now, don't you reckon you owe us some sort o' explanation ... some sort o' thank you? You ain't beyond that, are you, kid?'

Josey appreciated Ansel's claim, but he stared back stubbornly.

Finney Proud then stepped up close. 'You reckon we ain't above tossin' you right back where you just came from?' he said quietly.

Josey sniffed with irritation. 'Do you rangers reckon it was Lew Cayne who held up the stage?' he asked. 'Down at Kickin' S, you said you weren't sure,' he continued, looking at Ansel. 'Well, I know it wasn't him. An' maybe it wasn't *him* that should have gone to the pen.'

He didn't say any more because Remigo came riding back from his tracking along the rim of the arroyo.

'Our prairie cock's got himself a horse that's *still* favourin' its right foreleg,' the ranger reported with a wry smile. 'That sure makes him one busy son-of-a-bitch.'

Remigo's comments made it even more fascinating to hear what else Josey Minch had to say. But the ranger hadn't finished.

'An' I'm bein' followed,' he said. 'Nothin' hostile, just keepin' their distance, but they're comin' this way.'

Josey reached out and touched Ansel's arm.

'Maybe it's Mimms,' he muttered.

Ansel threw him an unbelieving, swift glance, then jerked his head at Remigo and Finney, indicated that they circle out to the left and right of him and Josey. If it was someone coming after Josey, Ansel wanted to be there, and he drew his Colt in anticipation.

As they waited, Ansel wondered why Josey would think that Clarke Mimms was riding through the night. He was considering an innocent sounding way of asking, when Finney Proud's voice cut through the darkness.

'Comin' in, Ansel. There's three of us, so hold your fire,' he called out the approach warning.

Like Finney, when he'd first seen Lew Cayne enter the saloon in Hackberry, Ansel knew instinctively who the third man was.

Under the moonlight, Ansel could see that the man's features were still raw from the fight that he'd had with Morton Frome.

Covered by the rifles of Finney and Remigo, Cayne sat his horse calmly. He was making no attempt to escape or cause trouble, and his bruised face remained impassive, until he caught sight of Josiah Minch. Then he gave a short, sharp smile of concern.

'Josey, what the hell are you doin' here?' he asked.

The boy's glance went swiftly from one face to another. 'I was ridin' to warn you that Mimms knows where you're hangin' out,' he said, instantly aware that he'd incriminated himself.

Cayne stared back at him for a moment, and then spoke quietly. 'I'm guessin' all three o' you are rangers,' he said. 'Bearin' in mind the nature o' the law in these parts, I'm sort've hopin' you're goin' to be more fair-minded with it.'

'Er, yeah, we'd like to think we have been

so far,' Ansel said, slightly taken aback.

'There's been a couple o' gunnies lyin' for me up at the shack,' Cayne said, and looked appreciatively towards Josey. 'I guess we can put *that* down to Clarke Mimms. You don't look so good, Josey,' he added. 'What the hell happened?'

'I got jumped. If it hadn't been for the Sholtos, an' the rangers here, I'd still be sniffin' the arroyo bed,' Josey answered.

'Why don't you get off that horse?' Ansel said.

Cayne glanced at the lowered guns and then dismounted.

'Yeah, tell us somethin' we don't know,' Finney suggested, pushing his rifle back into its saddle holster.

Cayne swung to the ground, let loose the reins of his horse. 'I'm no more the stage robber *now* than I was *ten years* ago,' he stated emphatically. 'I was framed then, an' it looks like the same dude's stickin' it to me again.'

Ansel reached into his pocket and brought out the snub-barrelled Colt with Cayne's carved initials. 'Well, *this* ain't a twist o' horehound candy,' he said. 'It was left behind in the coach.'

Cayne stared at the gun. 'It's a nice-lookin' piece. But these letters could've been chiselled by anyone with a pocket knife. They ain't exactly bespoke, an' it's nothin' I'd want, if that's what you're suggestin'. Ten years ago, it was a couple o' gold bars stashed in my saddle traps. I wonder what kind o' stunt they'll think up next?'

'I doubt there'll ever be one,' Ansel said, putting the gun back in his pocket. 'But tell me, Cayne, why come back here if you *didn't* hold up the stage? If you'd gone somewhere's else, there'd be someone *there* to say so, if you get my meanin'.'

'I know what you're sayin', Ranger. But there's two reasons: one, I didn't know the stage was bein' held up, an' *two,* why the hell shouldn't I? I've got to say them things *here,* not *somewhere's else.*'

Ansel smiled. 'Go on,' he said encouragingly.

'Ten years ago, Wallace Egham was bribed to say he'd seen me. It didn't take a lot to work out who was behind it all ... them that was of a mind, an' capable. Clarke Mimms, Morton Frome, Egham an' maybe one or two others. But it's Mimms I want, an' I want him in Yuma. Preferably, the same goddamn cell.'

Ansel could sense more fingers of guilt pointing towards Clarke Mimms. And wasn't *he* the main reason for Governor Degger bringing the rangers to Hackberry in the first place? 'An' young Josey's been helpin' with that mission o' yours, has he?' he asked.

'Yeah. I've served my time, so that ain't yet an offence.'

Ansel nodded in agreement. 'So Mimms knew you were comin' back?'

'Yeah, he knew. I heard him,' Josey broke in.

'I made no secret of it,' Cayne said. 'Some-one must've got word out to Mimms, an' he thought he'd pull the same goddamn stunt, ten years on. Ha. If it had been someone else, I'd have admired it.'

'Did you know that Josey was friendly towards Mimms?' Ansel asked. He watched for a reaction, his eyes flitting from Cayne to Josey.

'Set a thief to catch a thief or some such, eh, Ranger? Well you can forget *that* line,' Cayne responded. 'Josey knows better than that. He's lived here all these years, don't forget, an' young 'uns got eyes an' ears too. Now, Josey's playin' Mimms for the sucker he is: it ain't the other way round.'

But Ansel hadn't been forgetting or over-looking anything. His thoughts had been running along similar lines. 'You been playin' Buck Scarlett for a sucker, too?' he asked Josey.

Josey nodded. 'Yeah, I had to,' he said. 'I had to let them all think I was a dumb kid.'

11

'There's one thing that interests *me*,' Finney Proud said, looking hard at Lew Cayne. 'If Mimms framed you ten years ago, what's his beef *now?* Why start the whole darn thing over again?'

Cayne shrugged disconsolately. 'Well, I have given it *some* thought, an' I don't know what or why.'

'I think I do,' Remigo said, who'd been watching Cayne very closely. 'He learned o' you gettin' out o' the Yuma pen, an' got kind o' frightened ... still is.'

Ansel nodded, raised a chilly smile. 'Yeah, he's thinkin' ten years to pay for. So he gets you dragged straight back, an' picks up a small fortune in gold to compensate for the fear you caused him. Nice convenient package, eh, fellers?'

'Yeah, perhaps we can tell him now,' Finney suggested.

'Tell me *what?*' Cayne asked.

'That we didn't come to Hackberry because o' *you*,' Ansel responded. 'There's no doubt that Mimms is implicated, but it's cattle rustlin' that got us here. You've just muddied the waters.'

'But takin' most stuff into account, you're goin' along on the possibility that I'm innocent?' Cayne anticipated.

'Yeah, travellin' with it,' Ansel supported with a wry smile. 'Someone's got to start believin' what they hear sometime, If it's us, maybe we can save some time.'

Believing they were getting somewhere, Josey alleged that Sheriff Teach was taking orders from Mimms, reckoned he was being blackmailed, and was taking money.

The rangers were more interested now. If something like that was happening, it was more likely to have aroused the attention and suspicions of Governor Degger.

There was Simon Quinnel to be considered too. Not only for the planted Colt, but that him and Teach were living at Hackberry when Cayne went to the pen. Curious too, that both of them had been definite about Mimms being a solid citizen. Josey and Cayne couldn't add much, but Ansel wasn't going to ignore the town's good doctor, just yet.

'What about the cove who broke into the Kickin' S?' Finney asked.

No one was still any the wiser, and they shrugged or shook their heads.

'We know more about his goddamn *mount*,' Remigo put in.

Josey put his fingertips to his throat. 'The man's a likely killer, we know *that*,' he exclaimed.

'An' what about *this?* You reckon you could've lost it, Josey?' Ansel said, holding up the soap-tablet-sized gold bar. 'It was near to where you were lyin'.'

Josey smiled tiredly. 'Buck always learned me not to lose gold bars,' he joked. 'Apart from that, I never seen it before in my life.'

With a half smile, Cayne stepped in to take a closer look. 'This ain't the same bullion they planted on me; I ain't forgettin' what I saw in court,' he said. 'The Wolf Hole was usin' two triangles linked by a circle. This stamp's got three linked triangles.'

Josey resolved that. 'They changed their trademark,' he said. 'They changed the wolf's head.'

'When was that?' Ansel asked.

'I'm not sure; I just remember Buck sayin' at the time. He said the first one always did look more like a pig.'

Ansel continued to stare at the gold bar. 'Well, if it ain't from a ten-year-old lode, maybe it's part of our recent raid,' he said, his mind suddenly working on an idea.

'Are you goin' after Mimms?' Josey wanted to know.

Ansel looked up from the gold bar's imprint. 'Sure, but not in the way your mind's workin',' he said, tucking the bar into one of his saddle-bags. 'There's no proof that Mimms framed Lew. You got to bear in mind that the law's for everybody, gooses an' ganders.'

'Fair enough,' Cayne said. Then he was suddenly attracted by what Josey was doing. The youngster had stepped close to the edge of the arroyo, was looking down into the gloom.

'There's more gold, an' now I know where it's hidden,' he said and a meaningful grin crossed his face.

Josey led the riders to the end of the arroyo. There, where the old watercourse had once slipped underground they'd turned back along the dried-out river-bed. An hour later they reined in close to where Josey had fallen from the rim that was now above them.

'If there is gold stashed anywhere near here, this is where it'll be. I should have thought of it before. It's the obvious place,' he said excitedly.

'Shouldn't take us long to find out,' Remigo said, brandishing one of the brushwood torches that they'd collected on their journey. 'What you remember as a kid's only half the size when you're fully grown. It's probably nothin' more'n a cottontail's burrow.'

'No, you just follow me,' Josey said, and went to where an overhang of rock ran shadowy along the bottom side of the arroyo wall. 'Keep your heads down. I remember the roof ain't too solid.'

'Thanks for that, Josey, but me an' Finney will take it up from here,' Ansel said. 'You stay here with Remigo an' Lew. Remigo keeps watch, in case someone returns to finish the job they started earlier. When Mimms discovers his murderous little scheme's failed, he won't want to pussyfoot around. I don't want us all in one spot if that happens.'

Ansel and Finney moved along the old cut-back watercourse, passed through an alcove where the darkness became intense. They went on, deeper through another stretch of hollowed out tunnel, then into a larger cavern. Ansel stopped to light a second torch as Finney's flickered and died.

'What the hell are we doin' down here, Ansel?' Finney asked, but not expecting an answer.

The crackling, yellow light flickered, picked out something in the dust ahead of them. Finney picked it up, pinched a fat cigar butt between his thumb and forefinger. 'Ain't been here long, an' it sure don't belong to any one o' them Sholtos,' he said wryly.

Ansel was then holding his torch at arm's length, looking around the walls of the cavern. 'What the hell brought *that* down here?' he said, indicating a silt-dusted box that had been wedged into a deeply scoured pocket.

Ansel and Finney laid their torches alongside the box. Then they dragged it down to the ground, where Finney pulled the slatted top off to reveal the contents of five smaller bullion carriers. They were all empty, except the one that contained gold bars impressed with the Wolf Hole's triangles and circle brand.

'Looks like we struck our very own Comstock Lode, *compadre*,' Finney exclaimed.

'Yeah, thanks to young Josey,' Ansel said. 'It's about what I'd guess we'd find. I just wasn't sure where.'

'But from what Cayne was tellin' us, this is from the old haul. None of it bears that new Wolf Hole brand,' Finney said. 'An' there's probably nothin' else down here, except goddamn vampire bats.'

'So where in the name o' Sam Hill did the one I picked up, come from?' Ansel questioned.

'I don't know, Ansel. Let's just get the hell out o' here.'

12

The following evening, Buck Scarlett stood in the back parlour of his Kicking S ranch house. He'd just come back from a trip out to the ranch's dry goods barn. It was where animal feed, grain and perishable foodstuffs were stored on the edge of the home pasture; where Lew Cayne was presently quartered. Having been advised to move from the miner's shack up near the Sholtos' cabin, Cayne had been taken there with food and drink earlier in the day. He also had Remigo Correa as discreet, protective company.

Scarlett had spoken with Cayne. After ten years he'd been summarily touched and remorseful. He still was, as he talked with Ansel Agnes, Finney Proud and his ward Josiah Minch.

'I don't rightly know what to say to you fellers,' he said with rare diffidence. 'You must know how I feel. Lew Cayne was as close to me as any son could be. It's a mixed blessin' to know that he *wasn't* guilty. I guess it never was more than a half belief.'

A slight, quizzical look flitted across Ansel's face. He wondered how the close feelings only added up to a half belief.

But that confidence in Cayne's innocence, that he'd been framed by Clarke Mimms, only helped to get Scarlett's co-operation with the rangers' plan. The rancher had ensured that Kicking S hands were well out of the way when Cayne was relocated there.

During his earlier meeting with Scarlett, Cayne had waved aside any mutual regrets, or grievances, even bearing in mind that, at the trial, Scarlett had said or done very little to ascertain Cayne's innocence.

'If only I'd seen what was ahead of it all, maybe things would have been different,' Scarlett had said.

'Yeah maybe. But if our foresight was as

good as our hindsight, we'd never make mistakes, an' Christ, wouldn't that be borin'?' Cayne had responded with no apparent ill feeling. 'All the same, I'm mighty pleased to know you don't think I was guilty, Buck. It's never too late eh?'

Scarlett had conceded and nodded half-heartedly. 'It's funny that once folk accepted you were the hold-up man, I got to thinkin' it too ... just took it for granted. It's for *that* I'm sorry, Lew. Real sorry,' he'd said.

But now Scarlett was back at the ranch, and he looked from Ansel to Josey.

'An' I reckon there's an apology for you too, Josey,' he conceded. 'I thought you were playin' the village idiot with Mimms. Looks like it was the other way round.' Scarlett delivered a thin, rueful smile. 'There's no fool like an old one, they say.'

Josey shrugged. 'I don't know about that,' he said. 'Maybe I ought to have told you what I was really doin'. I wanted to play the hand on my own. I didn't think you'd go along with thinkin' Lew was innocent. An' I didn't like pretendin' about Mimms, either. "No fool like a young un" eh, Pa?'

'I don't want to be the one to hobble any real family feelin' here,' Ansel said, 'but we got to get movin'.' To the ranger, most things were falling into place, building up a neat picture of what *had* and what *was* happening in Hackberry. With the exception of the thieving from the Kicking S.

Buck Scarlett was watching the ranger, trying to estimate his thoughts. 'You goin' to try an' bluff Mimms?' he asked.

'Yeah, why not? We got no reason to suppose that Mimms is on to Josey,' Ansel said turning to the youngster. 'But if *you* reckon there's any chance of him sussin' you out, just say so. We'll work on somethin' else.'

Josey considered it for a short moment. 'Naagh, I reckon it'll be OK,' he said. 'Even if the galoot who jumped me is one o' Mimms's boys, he's still got no reason to suspect me.'

'OK, Josey, get yourself back to Hackberry. At least it'll be the truth to say you don't know what happened. Say every-body's lashin' out first an' askin' questions afterwards. Blame it on Cayne an' the robberies, then spin him the tale. That should make some sort o' sense.'

'Yeah, you watch out, Josey,' Scarlett said. 'Mimms obviously ain't a man to keep gettin' fooled. Just carry on actin' the spoilt dumb kid,' he added, with an affectionate smile.

Trying to get a handle on the events, Finney eyed Ansel, then Buck Scarlett. 'Right, let's get this clear,' he said. 'Cayne's told you he's innocent, an' that he's got proof of it. For ol' times' sake, you believe him, an' are lettin' him squat on your land?'

Scarlett and Ansel nodded as Finney con-tinued. 'Cayne's goin' to hand over that proof to the rangers – that's us – but not until tomorrow, because tonight we're *sup-posed* to be ridin' north, still on the trail of the Gemmer gang. Cayne's on his lonesome, but o' course he ain't. Remigo's there with him, an' we'll be joinin' 'em afore they both get capped. How's that?'

'Yeah, that's about it, Finney,' Ansel agreed. 'O' course, there's always a chance that Mimms won't fall for Josey's story, but we've agreed it's a chance worth takin'. Mimms is a card player. Let's hope he sees the odds that way.'

'Tell me about the gold,' Scarlett asked. 'It was–' But he stopped suddenly and held up his hand for quiet. He went to a window and looked out across the yard. 'Yeah, I thought I heard somethin',' he said. 'One o' the hands has got himself a wolf pup. Sounds like he's in the bunkhouse, an' they're out clearin' mesquite from the corrals. The mutt's probably tearin' the place to bits. Either that, or I'm gettin' jittery.'

'Ferocious little tykes are enough to make anyone jittery,' Ansel said. 'But you were goin' to ask about the gold,' he reminded him.

'Oh yeah. You reckon Mimms had it hidden there for ten years?'

'It didn't look like it had been anywhere

else. An' it couldn't have been long after Josey an' his pals had stopped playin' around there. He probably thought it safer than keepin' it in his hotel or the Sweet Gold ranch.'

'What have you done with it?' Scarlett asked, then smiled at the thought of Ansel telling him.

'What was left of it, you mean?' and Ansel smiled back at the gaffe.

The ranger was still wondering how the gold bar he'd found on the arroyo bed had got there. Whoever had robbed the ranch, was a dilemma too. Unless it was as Josey had said at the time, the work of an opportunist drifter. But Ansel was sure of one thing: the gold robberies, the cattle rustling and Clarke Mimms were now all in the same file of enquiry. He also thought that with so little to go on and no hard facts, maybe blackmail was playing a part. By its very nature, it was a crime with little obvious publicity or evidence.

'You can get goin' now, kid,' he advised

Josey. 'But stay *here* when you get back.'

Some time later, Ansel and Finney rode up to the Sholtos' shack. It was on the way to where Lew Cayne was holed up at the Kicking S barn. Finney heeled his mount to one side, thought he'd take a look around the parcel of land.

'I've come to talk to you boys about them reward dollars,' Ansel called out, on approaching the boys who were already standing outside their cabin. 'But I said I'd be needin' extra information.'

'It's for what we *did*, nothin' more,' Jack answered back defiantly.

'I told you terms at the time, kid. Now I ain't got time to negotiate, so you take it or leave it. Tell me why Howard Teach wanted you out o' the way so quick, back at the Kickin' S'

'We saw him talkin' to a feller out beyond the creek. Sheriff saw us, but we pretended we hadn't seen *him*.'

'An' that's it?' Ansel questioned sharply.

'No. He came back. He was here a while ago. Wanted to know if we *did* see him. We said we didn't know what he was talkin' about. Don't know whether he believed us or not, but he was a mite scratchy about somethin'.'

'*Did* you know this man he was talkin' to? Or seen him before?'

'Yeah, it was Dougal Bleat, one o' the Sweet Gold waddies.'

Ansel pulled a roll of five, ten-dollar bills from his top pocket, handed it down to Bryn Sholto. 'There's fifty dollars. Why don't you tell us the real story o' what it was you were doin' out there, besides bundlin' up firewood,' he suggested, with a mischievous smirk.

Bryn turned to his brother, but before they could come up with something, Finney rode in.

'There's someone here rides a horse that's favourin' its right foreleg,' he said. 'What do you say to that, Ansel?'

'I'd say the money I just paid out buys us

a look inside this here fleapit.'

The twins stood close to each other listening and watching while Ansel dismounted in front of their cabin.

'Where's your ma?' he asked them.

'Tombstone,' Bryn answered directly. 'She said it was to visit her sister, but she won't be back.'

'Hmm. Keep an eye on 'em,' Ansel advised Finney before going in. 'I've seen 'em run.'

Ansel was only gone for a short time. He wasn't that surprised at what was lying around, what was stacked before his eyes, and the feral stench. He found what he was looking for in the first place he looked. Under the crock of pine-top whiskey lay Buck Scarlett's $2,000.

'We got a visitor,' Finney called out.

But Ansel was already watching from the stoop, saw Simon Quinnel riding towards them on his sturdy-built mare.

The doc held in any unease he might have had, looked from the twins to Finney and Ansel.

'One person for every thousand acres, the Eastern newspapers tell you,' he said, with a guarded smile. 'Wonder why it is then, that all of a sudden you get five of 'em in the same goddamn spot?'

'Don't know, Doc, perhaps it should be you with an explanation. Failin' that, tell us exactly what you were doin' out at the Kickin' S, when Scarlett lost his cash money.'

'We were playin' poker. Five card stud, exactly. Why'd you want to know?' Quinnel asked.

'Rangers are naturally inquisitive I guess ... nosy if you like. So you rushed out with 'em did you, when the commotion started?'

'Yeah ... well, perhaps not right off. Weren't goin' to leave Buck's fine whiskey behind.'

Ansel smiled. 'No, o' course not,' he said, with some understanding.

13

Clarke Mimms sat behind his office desk at the Rincon Roost. It was evening, and nearly twenty-four hours had elapsed since he'd talked with Frome after the fight with Lew Cayne. There hadn't been much that had gone right since.

'We've got no idea where Cayne is now,' Frome rasped anxiously. '*He* must know by now that we set him up, an' we know he's out there gettin' set to do somethin' about it. We've got enough stashed away in Nogales, so why the hell don't we get down there while we still can?'

Mimms said nothing, he was thinking about what Cayne had said to Morton Frome. And word had gone round Hackberry that the rangers were doubting it was Lew Cayne who'd staged the recent hold-up. The second attempt to frame him had failed, and up at the old miner's shack, Egham and Bleat had missed their chance to silence him once and for all.

'He ain't goin' to let up,' Frome continued. 'He's had ten years chewin' away inside him. He probably ain't got nothin' left but bile. We can't sit here waitin' for him.'

Again Mimms said nothing. He was thinking about a contingency plan when someone knocked falteringly on his door. At a nod from Mimms, Frome turned the key in the lock, pulled open the door and confronted Wallace Egham and Dougal Bleat, who were waiting, tense and nervous.

Mimms stared at the men coldly. He wasn't pleased that they'd slipped up the previous night. Egham would presumably have done his best to get the man who was seeking revenge, but he'd failed. Bleat hadn't joined the Mimms outfit until some years after the robberies. He was a hired gun, had come with a reputation for being efficient and tough.

'What do you two want?' he challenged, as the men came into his office.

'We don't like the way things are goin',' Egham answered. 'You never told us there were goin' to be rangers snoopin' around. We're up against too many, an' we want out.'

'Those goddamn rangers are after the Gemmer gang. That ain't no secret,' Mimms said intolerantly.

'Well now it's us they're interested in,' Bleat countered.

'An' who the hell's fault's that?' Mimms spluttered with rising anger. The way things were, only Egham, Frome and himself knew, or were supposed to know, what had happened ten years ago. For that reason, he wasn't best pleased that Egham was losing his nerve. Bleat had been told that Mimms wanted Lew Cayne out of the way because he didn't want him coming back to Hackberry and staging any more robberies. Gunmen weren't normally paid to think things through. But if Egham's nerve was going, and he'd talked to Bleat, who else? 'Sounds to *me*, like you been chewin' things over with Bleat,' he said with clear irritation.

But it was Bleat who answered. 'I don't need him speakin' for me,' he said. 'I got to wonderin' what was goin' on, an' now I know. I didn't know about any rangers bein' involved, either. They don't give up easy ... get paid to run you down. So if they're makin' time to ride north after the Gemmers, I reckon that's the time to ride on.'

Mimms stared hard at the gunman. He knew there was more to it than the man turning tail and running, and he was right.

'Just give me some ground money, an' I'll forget I ever heard anythin',' Bleat suggested. 'I ain't sittin' around here waitin' for trouble. Whatever Egham wants, that's up to him.'

Mimms opened his desk drawer an inch, considered lifting out both derringers and killing Bleat there and then. What more trouble could he be in? Mimms had always estimated that Wallace Egham was smart enough, albeit disagreeable and mean-spirited. For nearly ten years, Mimms had maintained Egham's compliance with a cash payment or lumber contract. It was the accepted price for his faked evidence when Cayne was brought to trial.

Mimms slammed the drawer shut as Frome took a threatening step towards Egham and Bleat.

'No, leave 'em,' he snapped. 'Ground money's what they pay rodeo cowboys, ain't it, when no one wins?' Mimms gave Bleat a pinched smile. 'Very apt,' he said. 'Come back in half an hour.'

Bleat's eyes narrowed with concern. 'I was reckonin' on now. I've done enough waitin' in this town.'

'I said half an hour, 'cause I had good reason,' Mimms said, as a clear ultimatum.

Bleat hesitated, then turned to the door. 'No harm in tryin',' he sniffed. 'I'll be back.'

Mimms suggested that Frome found some alternative distraction until he called him back. 'An' take *him* with you, before he says somethin' he regrets,' he added, indicating Egham. 'Buy him a drink. I've got somethin' to see to.'

It was all paid work to Frome, not too disagreeable, and he pushed Egham out towards the bar. But Egham sidestepped, took a quick couple of steps back into Mimms's office. 'I got somethin' to tell you,' he said. 'Might be worth knowin'.'

'Knowin' *what?*' Mimms demanded.

'The kid was hangin' around here last night. I saw him in the alley, snoopin' furtive like. He took off when he heard me comin'. I thought maybe you'd want to know ... keep it in mind for the next time you see him.'

'Yeah, I will. Anythin' more?' Mimms asked.

'No, just that. Don't forget he knew Cayne. He was nothin' more'n a button, but he woulda been mighty influenced.'

'Thanks, yeah. I guess you mean long lastin'. Get back to the bar with Mort, an' don't move too far.'

Mimms sat himself back down and waited. He opened his drawer again, this time a little more than an inch. Seeing the ivory handles of the matched derringers made him feel more confident.

Ten minutes later, the light began to fade. He lit his table lamp and pulled the window blind. Then he opened the door and left it slightly ajar, sat back down and continued his wait.

'I sniffed some mighty interestin' wind up at the Kickin S,' his visitor said, as he slipped quietly into the office a short while later.

'I'll decide whether it's interestin'. Just tell me what you heard,' Mimms snapped impatiently, and listened to what the man had to tell him.

'Sounds like Mort's got the right idea,' he muttered, as soon as his informer had gone. Then he swore vehemently. The rangers were on to him, so he wouldn't be livin' out his days in Hackberry. The money he'd got banked across the border would keep him in comfort for as long as he wished, but it wasn't the way he'd planned it, and he cursed again. But he'd got some time left to make the most of, to consider what to do about young Josey Minch.

He went into the saloon and gave Frome the nod, indicated that he bring Egham back with him. He also saw the sheriff, reckoned he'd be there for a while yet.

'I reckon you were right about young Minch,' he said to Egham. 'He's in with the rangers, and they're in with Cayne, an' they're after you an' me both.'

'So what we do? What do *I* do?' Egham asked, in a rising, shrilly voice.

'Keep your head for a start. Just do as I tell you.'

'Well, *tell* it for Chris'sake, 'cause I ain't got plans for a like situation.'

'The kid's on his way here. You do it anyway you want, but see to it that he don't get to go anywhere else *after* that. You do that, Wally, 'cause if you don't ... well...' Mimms let the ominous words hang in the air. As one of the men responsible for framing Lew Cayne, and for perjuring himself in court, Egham didn't need any convincing on the intent of any headstrong youngster.

Mimms let himself out of his second office door, came out behind the saloon bar and picked a bottle of decent whiskey from the shelf below the bar top. He took it to where Howard Teach was sitting, sat down and refilled the man's glass.

'Evenin', Sheriff. You got keys to that legalized arsenal o' yours?' he asked briefly.

'I always carry 'em, yeah.'

'You still got the dynamite you took from them claim jumpers?'

The sheriffs rheumy eyes narrowed. 'Yeah,' he said, 'why?'

'I'd like the keys for a bit, if you don't mind. An' you don't mind, do you, Howard?' he suggested with an icy smile.

Teach seemed to shrink at that moment. The tip of his tongue ran around his lips, added some moisture to the dryness of fear. He pulled out his keys looked at them and handed them over.

Mimms took them and put them straight in his pocket. He nodded. 'Work your way through *this*,' he said, meaning the bottle of whiskey.

14

When Josey Minch entered the Rincon Roost, Wallace Egham rocked back on his heels, sat with his back against the wall.

'If you want a hand o' blackjack, I could relieve you o' some soft-earned dollars,' he sneered, from his table. 'Seems almost everyone else in town's had the chance.'

'That's 'cause I *like* most everyone else,' Josey answered back readily.

Josey tried to pit his long-held dislike for the lumber-yard owner against the desire to win a few hands of cards. But the chance to take Egham's money won out, and Josey fell in. With the toe of his boot, he dragged a chair towards him and sat down.

'That's the trouble with hayseeds,' Egham said, as he refilled his whiskey glass. 'They're mostly losers ... chancers tryin' to win back their losses.'

Josey smiled bleakly. 'Not like *you* then, Egham?' he retorted. 'Sittin' here on your own, just waitin' for one of 'em to come along so's you can make another dollar. Yessir, that's when you know you've really hit the big time.'

Egham ground his teeth as he dealt a card for Josey and one for himself.

Josey had a look at his card, saw the King of Spades. I'm being suckered, he thought, and, the next card's going to be part of a winning hand. I'm *young* he thought, but not *stupid*.

Egham raised an eyebrow and a small, spittled smile when Josey pushed a ten-dollar bill across the table. Yeah, that's it, Josey thought, as the Queen of Spades went down as his face up card. He took an involuntary breath, wondered what Egham's game was. He placed another ten on top of the first, allowed himself a smile back at the dealer. He was going to take a third card. The odds were well stacked against him that he'd bust, but it would surprise and throw Egham if he had fixed the deal.

If he'd had it on him, Josey would have staked a month's allowance on the third card being an ace. 'I just have to do this,' he said, fingering another ten dollars. 'I'll buy me a third.'

'Yep, thought so,' he gasped, as Egham overlapped the Queen with the Ace of Spades. 'It's got to be a family thing.'

Egham bust his hand with a nine, and Josey showed his twenty-one. 'Ma an' Pa an' their button,' he said with barely concealed glee.

'Don't believe I've ever seen that done before.' Egham's voice was a leery whisper. 'Takin' a third on two courts.'

'Just testin' my luck,' Josey asserted. 'It looks like maybe it's in, so let's go again.'

On the next hand, Egham stayed with nineteen, and Josey hit him with a queen and a ten. Within minutes Josey was nearly fifty dollars up and wondering when his luck was supposed to run out.

Josey lifted a card, took a longer look as if he didn't want to make a mistake on his bet. He smiled and looked around him. 'Where's Sheriff Teach?' he asked casually. 'It ain't like him to miss a deal, 'specially when there's a loaded hayseed in town, eh, Mr Egham?'

'He *was* here. He must've had a more pressin' engagement,' Egham said. The lumber merchant was wondering what Josey's real intentions were, thinking on Clarke Mimms's instructions.

Mimms had been in his office for nearly a half-hour before Frome mentioned Josey. 'He's been here a short while. He's had a few hands with Egham ... actually looks to be on some sort o' run. His return ain't ever been more'n ten cents on the dollar, so it almost seems a shame to break it up. It ain't house money he's takin'.'

'Hmm. Go have a word with him, before he comes stompin' in here,' Mimms replied.

Frome walked straight across the saloon

towards Josey. 'Boss wants to see you,' he said, taking Josey a bit by surprise. 'If you follow me, he's through here.'

'Oh, OK. Seems a shame to fold on a winnin' streak, but I reckon I've won the few hands I was suckered for,' Josey said. He turned and gave Egham a brief but meaningful smile, then went after Frome through to the back bar.

Josey was alert, but he wasn't yet expecting any danger. 'Why are we goin' this way?' he asked.

'He's closed up the other door. There was always some goddamn nuisance folk tryin' to see him. This way keeps some protection ... keeps 'em at arm's length.'

Josey was taking it in, getting suspicious, when Egham moved quickly to hit him. The man punched him hard in the back of the neck and sent him reeling. Frome kicked at his legs, pushed him into Mimms's office and slammed the door to.

'This'll be the game you lose tonight, kid,' Mimms rasped, as Josey stumbled and fell heavily to the floor.

Josey didn't say anything because his neck was locked solid with pain. But he was thinking, wondering what had happened, what had gone wrong. As he dragged himself to his knees, he knew. It hadn't been any wolf pup that Buck had heard out at the ranch. It was someone tripping over the parlour's trash cans in their haste to get away with Clarke Mimms's information.

15

Up at the Sholto house, Ansel and Finney watched Simon Quinnel ride back in the direction of Hackberry. The doctor said that he was doing his rounds, thought he'd better call in on Cob to look at a bite wound the man had got from a snared badger a few days previously. But with Cob's absence, it was obvious he was at least walking wounded. Quinnel prescribed that as a hopeful sign, and decided to get on his way.

Finney laughed, said for the doc to go and check out the poor badger.

Ansel, too, was wondering on the whereabouts of Cob Sholto. Judging by the evidence of the horse's foreleg, the man had robbed Buck Scarlett. And maybe he'd been working alone, not on Clarke Mimms's orders. Having told Finney about the dollars he'd found in the cabin, Ansel decided to have another talk with the twins.

'I'm guessin' you two don't get along with your old man?' he said, not unkindly.

'There ain't much to get along with.' It was Bryn who spoke, and his face showed little emotion.

'Yeah, that's the impression I got. But he could be puttin' both o' you in a tricky ol' place. Why not talk to us, an' we'll see if there's a way out?' Ansel didn't want to come between a father and his sons, but he had to ask.

'Last night we weren't out collectin' wood,' Jack said, after a glance at Bryn. 'We was watchin' someone. He's the one broke into the Kickin' S. We didn't have any difficulty followin' him.'

Ansel nodded slow and deliberately. No, you wouldn't, if he was your pa, he thought to himself. But that was as much as the twins would admit to. There was still some curious Sholto loyalty. 'Do you know anythin' else that might be useful to us?' he asked.

'Why don't you take a ride back along the crick an' find out?' Bryn said.

Ansel presumed the boys had been suspicious about their pa's activities for some time. Instinct and cunning wasn't one of their family failings.

Now things were fitting together. A lot of them were pointing in the same direction, and Ansel decided to make a move by riding out with Finney to the Kicking S ranch house. Clarke Mimms wouldn't make a move yet; it was only just approaching first dark and Song Creek was on the way to where the rangers would be rendezvousing with Remigo and Lew Cayne.

Ansel and Finney rode hurriedly for the arroyo. Finney reckoned a serious chance was being taken by acting on Bryn Sholto's suggestion. 'Only bad things happen out there,' he said, with understandable concern.

Eventually, Ansel had to ask Finney if he knew where they were.

'No, but it can't be far away,' the ranger replied. 'I reckon we should leave the horses here an' walk real careful until we know we're there.'

Cob Sholto had been sitting for some time with his head between his knees. He was on the rim of the arroyo, wondering what to do next. He was so deeply into a mire of frustration that he failed to hear Ansel and Finney approaching. He shuddered, put up his hands nervously the moment he caught the sound of Finney's nearby footfall.

Finney stepped forward, quickly relieved him of his big, old Army Colt. 'Curious minin' style,' he said, noticing the rope that trailed down from its loop around Sholto's shoulders. 'You strike anythin' down there?'

'No, you didn't,' Ansel continued, before Sholto had time to respond. 'Because we moved it last night after I hauled the boy up from where you'd put him. You got somethin' against kids, have you?' he said, pushing the toe of his boot hard into the man's ribs. 'Got to worryin' when you found him gone, eh, weasel meat?'

Cob's face twisted into a hostile sneer, as he stared fearfully up at Ansel. He muttered, but the ranger took no notice.

'It was *you* relieved Buck Scarlett of two thousand dollars,' Ansel charged. 'Enough notes to pack up the base of a crock o' whiskey piss. Then you went into Hackberry an' talked to Clarke Mimms about Cayne bein' up at the old miner's shack. After that, you came here for the bullion and to lay out Josey Minch.' Ansel paused for a moment before adding, 'I'm hopin' that there really ain't any honour between thievin' factions, Cob.'

'What do you mean by that?'

'Tell us what we want to know, an' we'll let you ride that dish-wheeled nag o' yours out o' here.'

Sholto's persistently shifting eyes now steadied, tried to get behind Ansel's face, into his mind. 'How do I know that ain't to buffler me?' he asked.

''Cause we ain't all congenital liars,' Ansel snarled back. 'What we know about you's worth about five years inside. Make your choice.'

Just a few minutes later, Sholto had corroborated a few facts and suspicions. Now Ansel and Finney knew what they wanted to know, including how the bar of Wolf Hole gold had got into the arroyo, and how Sholto had laid in wait for Josey Minch, thinking it was *him* who was after the bullion.

'Talk to him, Finn,' Ansel said. 'Make him see sense.' Then he watched as his colleague quietly threatened Sholto about what would happen if the man attempted to ride off and warn anyone.

'Now get up,' Finney said. 'Make a move or a sound before full dark, an' all those bad things I promised *will* come true.'

'That's real good,' Ansel accepted readily. 'About as affecting a piece of advice as I've ever heard. Now you've got to get to that goddamn Rincon Roost. I ain't twiddlin' thumbs waitin' for Clarke Mimms to make a move. It'll have to be you goes to get him, Finn.'

Finney rode north-east, striking across country for Hackberry and Mimms's hotel. He kicked hard, was kind of hoping there were enough law abiders to act on the words and influence of one of the governor's appointed rangers.

He was at the end of the main street, when Howard Teach drifted out of the deep shadow of an alleyway. There was another figure who lurked behind him whom Finney recognized as Dougal Bleat, a gun-carrying waddy from the Sweet Gold ranch. He was the man whom the Sholto twins had seen talking with the sheriff in the foothills.

Finney automatically rested the heel of his right hand on the butt of his Colt.

'Hold up there,' Teach said. 'I've got to tell one o' you rangers that I'm gettin' a posse out.'

'Is that gettin' or got?' Finney asked quickly. 'More importantly for *what?* An' what's *he* doin' with you?'

'Bleat's been workin' with me,' Teach

replied. 'It's a long story, but now we're stringin' ol' Mimms along. There's already trouble at the Rincon, an' worse comin'. That's where the posse comes in. You too, if you want.'

Finney shook his head, tried to clear it of the uncertainty, what looked like a turn-about of allegiances and paymasters. Bleat was a Mimms employee, hired primarily for his gun and little else. But Howard Teach being on the straight and narrow wasn't convincing, and Finney thought he detected the merest waft of fear.

'Yeah, I want,' he said. 'Now one o' you better tell me about this trouble.'

16

On the floor in Clarke Mimms's office, Josey Minch was a bound and gagged prisoner. It seemed a long time since Mimms, Egham and Morton Frome had left him, but Josey had no idea how long. As he twisted and tugged at the ropes that bound his hands and feet, all he could think about was the hurt and frustration of Mimms and his cohorts getting away. He strained against the double rope around his chest, but he was tied in securely to the base of Mimms's big, heavy desk. It was moving to full dark when he slumped with fatigue, realizing the rangers couldn't have a way of knowing that Mimms was planning to escape across the border into Mexico.

The office was in pitch darkness and raw pain was stinging his skinned wrists, when

Josey heard the muffled, but unmistakable gun shot. Another cracked the silence, and then a clash of sound like men fighting and shouting from inside the saloon, or just outside of it.

Josey wrenched again at the ropes, but he could only move enough to face the door that led to the saloon's back bar. Whoever had tied the knots had made them fast. Josey was well secured and he had no way of knowing what was going on, or the reason for it.

A third shot sounded much closer, then someone's boots pounded in the narrow passageway. The office door was kicked open, and Finney Proud entered, brandishing his carbine.

'Take it easy, kid, the cavalry's here,' he said. 'Whoever's done this, has got you well an' truly hog-tied.' The ranger pulled out a clasp knife and cut through the neckcloth that was tied around Josey's mouth, then the ropes that bound the rest of his body.

'Thank you,' Josey gasped, and took in a

deep draught of air. 'Maybe it was someone who ties down boards to the beds o' lumber wagons,' he said, his mouth sore and thickly parched.

Finney looked thoughtful for a short moment. 'Well, we've got Mimms cornered, but I'm reckonin' on—' He suddenly stopped talking, grabbed up his carbine and stepped back to one side of the open door as another gun exploded. A shard of wood splintered away from the door frame and the bullet buried itself in the wall above and behind Josey.

'Get down behind the desk,' Finney shouted, and Josey rolled across the floor. The movement shook some life back into the youngster and Finney threw his Colt to him, slid it across the floor between the pillars of the desk.

Josey caught a glimpse of someone crouched outside of the doorway and he knew it was Clarke Mimms. He supported himself on both elbows and levelled the Colt, drew back the hammer and fired. The gunshot crashed out, billowed an acrid, cordite cloud beneath the desk. As Josey rolled away he cursed, saw that Finney was getting himself set for taking a leap at Mimms.

'I'm goin' for him,' Finney yelled as he ran, lunging through the doorway.

Mimms glared, almost spat defiance at the ranger as he levelled out a shiny-plated derringer.

But Finney was moving too fast. He swung the carbine by its barrel, and the stock cracked solidly against the clutch of Mimms's fingers. The man yelled in pain, rolled into the space between the end of the bar and his own office door.

'Shoot him,' Mimms yelled for his men. But by that time Finney was standing over him with the tip of a carbine's barrel pressed hard into the flesh of his neck. Not one of the Mimms workforce had any desire to risk either Mimms's life or their own.

'Get to your feet,' Finney ordered. 'Get up an' back off towards me. I'm takin' you out o' here the way I came in. Any o' your crew think differently, they'll be in the employ of a dead man.'

Many townsfolk had already gathered in the main street. The watching crowd knew to keep their distance, but were milling at the sound of the shooting, eager in their witness to a gunfight. Sheriff Teach had organized his posse to form a picket around the hotel, and Josey noticed that Dougal Bleat was among them. Nearly all of the customers had now run from the saloon, but some firing continued. Gunshots were indiscriminate and erratically returned from the hotel's doors and windows.

After getting him out of the hotel, Finney edged Josey into cover. A bullet whined, kicked up dust at Finney's feet, then another as he threw himself around the corner of an adjoining building.

'We've got 'em penned in,' he muttered, 'but they ain't goin' to quit easy.'

Mimms was being held guard outside of the hotel's back door, but inside, a few of his men were still prepared to do battle. Finney and Teach had taken the Sweet Gold men by surprise, but now, and in their own interests, they were retaliating. Finney saw the huge bulk of Morton Frome; for a brief moment glimpsed him through one of the saloon's smashed windows. He'd suddenly appeared to take charge, Finney realized, and he moved from the corner of the building. He edged close to the wall and then quickly along the front of the hotel.

He turned into the alleyway, pushed against the door that led into the back bar of the saloon and Mimms's office. Those who'd been thinking of doing any shooting from there were now gone. Walking slow but sure, Finney reached the bar, only a couple of feet from where he'd struck Mimms. Ahead of him across the saloon, and firing out into the main street, Morton Frome was crouched by one of the front windows.

Finney rested his carbine across the wet slickered bar and drew back the hammer. At the sharp, ominous sound, Frome brought his gun hand down and slowly turned. Then he groaned, cursed at the sight of the man he was shooting at only a minute or so ago.

'Looks like we got this place to ourselves at last,' Finney rasped. 'Your round or mine?'

Frome gave the expected and ill-fated smile, then his fingers tightened around his Colt. But it was to little effect, and Finney pulled the trigger of his carbine. The bullet smashed out the leg of a nearby table and Frome gasped in shock, heaved his Colt towards the bar in angry surrender.

'Mine,' Finney confirmed icily. 'At your size, it would've taken someone a week to clean up all the blood, if you'd wanted a fight. Now move. If there's any of 'em left, I ain't waitin' for your cronies to come runnin' down them stairs.'

But from then on, the fight was over and the rest of Mimms's outfit caved in. Within minutes, the Rincon Roost and its customers were captive to the sheriff and his posse.

'Maybe we should be ridin' out to the Kickin' S,' Finney said, when he'd handed over Morton Frome. 'We done our part, but I reckon it ain't *all* over just yet.'

Josey Minch wasn't feeling so good. The youngster had endured a second night of ordeal, was bashed, bruised and racked with fatigue.

'Doc Quinnel ought to be takin' a look at you, kid, if you could find him.' Finney said. 'I reckon he's got somewhere else to be,' he added.

17

The roof of the dry goods barn shone pale under the moon. Remigo Correa and Lew Cayne had been holed-up since the afternoon, among the sacks of alfalfa and cotton cake. Ansel had ridden straight there when he'd left Song Creek. Knowing that Remigo would have him in his sights from a good vantage point, he'd approached cautiously when he got close.

'Where's Finney?' was the first thing Remigo asked, as he rode up.

'Hackberry. We had a talk with the Sholto boys, an' they gave us a lead on their pa. Well, a nod in the direction o' the arroyo. He won't be makin' any more trouble. Finney threatened him with sufferin's I ain't ever heard before.'

'Ain't just us mixed blood's got a

monopoly on that sort o' stuff then,' Remigo muttered. He was keeping watch from the window as Ansel brought him up to date. 'Well, here's *one* feller who might be lookin' to mix it with us. Either that, or we got ourselves a goddamn horse thief.'

Ansel moved in to take himself a look. 'Let him come on. It's a spider-an'-fly situation,' he said with quiet interest.

'He's against the dark. I can't tell who it is. I'll go outside an' find out if he's on his own,' Remigo decided.

Ansel doused the single lamp, and for five more minutes they waited in silence until they heard Remigo's voice.

'Almost had you down for a horse thief,' he called out.

Ansel swore quietly, flicked a match to relight the lamp. 'It's Buck Scarlett,' he said to Cayne. He stepped through the open door to see Remigo putting his Colt away. Scarlett dropped the reins of his horse that he'd walked for the last fifty yards.

'You come to check on your cattle cake?'

Ansel asked him, with an easy smile.

Scarlett shook his head. 'No,' he said. 'I was followin' someone from the ranch who must've come this way. An' they *did,* for so far.'

Immediately they were back in the barn, Ansel wanted to know who it was that Scarlett could have been on the trail of, what had happened.

'I was ridin' the close line, checkin' the ranch an' some o' the buildin's. I don't want another goddamn break-in,' Scarlett said, as he propped himself against a pile of sacked up maize. 'The boys were all in the bunk house by that time, but I saw one who wasn't. He was ridin' north, across the home pasture. Known' there ain't nothin' much out there, except this place, I thought maybe I'd ride along for a bit. I kept losin' him though. Under these goddamn clouds I never had more'n a minute or so of useful light. I got pretty close to here – maybe a half-mile out.'

Remigo nodded. 'Yeah, I saw you,' he said knowingly.

'Any idea who it *was?*' Cayne asked. 'At least we all know who it *wasn't.*'

'His mount was a big, broad-back. An' there's only one person I know rides one o' them.'

'Yeah, Hackberry's own saddle-bag doctor,' Ansel confirmed.

'Funny thing *is,* sometime earlier, one o' my boys mentioned he'd seen him out back of the house,' Scarlett said.

'It ain't *so* funny, Buck. It was Quinnel knew about the Colt that one o' these fellers found,' Cayne reminded them. 'He could've played a part in most all o' this?' he said thoughtfully.

Remigo indicated that he was going back outside. Ansel knew it was to have a scout around, to see if there was someone whom Scarlett followed to the barn.

'I reckon we should all get out there. Take advantage o' what's left o' the darkness,' Ansel advised. 'It looks like the clouds are movin' on. If someone's comin' an' we don't go now, we'll see *them* as they see *us.* Stay here, an' we get caught like fish in a barrel.'

Cayne moved over to the wall opposite the door and hunkered down. 'I'm stayin' put. I'll be facin' the door, so leave it open,' he said. 'If anyone comes through, they'll be well framed. Don't argue, I'm owed it.'

'Good. An' I'll get myself in the far corner. From there, I can keep an eye on *your* well-bein',' Scarlett said.

Ansel looked at Remigo and they accepted the arrangement as an ultimatum – arguably the due one.

'Let's go,' Ansel said, and the two rangers slipped into the darkness, Remigo silently tapping a wedge along the bottom of the open door.

Inside the barn, there was now no sound at all, except a slight, intermittent scratching from somewhere to Cayne's left. He smiled grimly, wondered how many generations of furred scavengers had clawed and gnawed eagerly, been frustrated by the brick foundations.

Then there was another sound, and Cayne

suddenly felt the sweat break out between his shoulder blades. He shuddered at the sound of a Colt's hammer being drawn back, its chamber clicking into place.

Cayne sighed with despair. He'd waited almost ten years for this moment, only to get most of it wrong. It was Buck Scarlett's gun, and the man was about to shoot him.

'The rangers are out there puttin' two an' two together,' he said, as calmly as he could. 'What you goin' to tell 'em, Buck?' Then he turned slow and careful until he was looking towards Scarlett. He saw the man's face, ashen grey from the weak moonlight that cut through the open doorway. He could also see the barrel of the Colt that pointed directly at him, the hard line of the finger that curled around the trigger.

'I'll think o' somethin',' Scarlett rasped coldly. 'I usually do when I've had time.' There was an immediate flash and crash of his gun firing, and a bullet hammered into the wall alongside Cayne's head.

But Cayne had instinctively measured the

timing of Scarlett's response and jerked to one side. Momentarily blinded and with his ears ringing, he straightened his gun arm and fired back. 'Not this time,' he yelled.

Within moments, Ansel had returned and was standing in the doorway. Scarlett fired again, but Ansel had leapt to one side, was shouting back at Remigo.

'Cover the door. There's only one way out.'

Cayne took the opportunity to move. He fired twice at where he thought Scarlett to be, cursed loudly and launched himself across the barn. Out of the corner of his eye he saw the shape of Ansel appear again as he grappled for Scarlett and his gun. He dropped his Colt to give him the use of both hands, clubbed down with his hands clasped tight together.

Scarlett was on his feet, when Cayne hit him. The two men fell to the dirt floor, and Cayne continued slamming his bunched fists into Scarlett's face and upper body.

Scarlett lay slumped on the floor as Cayne

snatched the Colt from the frenzied clutch of the defeated man's fingers. He was breathing heavy as he turned to pick up his own gun, thanked Ansel as the ranger handed it to him. He found it difficult to make much sense of the night's business, simply understood that Scarlett had intended to kill him. He was bemused, and he shook his head almost forlornly.

'Just imagine how young Josey's goin' to feel,' Ansel suggested thoughtfully. 'Take a hay bale, sit on it an' put the gun away. You won't have any more need of it this night.'

'I ain't finished yet, ranger. You're goin' to have to deal with my men,' Scarlett hissed, 'an' I'll be makin' real sure you do.'

'Aagh, shut it,' Ansel retorted. 'Your days o' sayin' what goes, are over. Stew awhile, an' I'll explain to everybody what you're doin' here.'

18

Ansel Agnes sniffed pensively. For the benefit of Lew Cayne, he was deciding on where to start his account of events following the robbery. He took a near hostile look at Buck Scarlett.

'You an' Mimms cached the gold at the arroyo cavern. You went back for it, bit by bit, so's not to arouse any suspicion, although it wouldn't have been such a smart move if the creek water had decided to wake up. Not gettin' on with Mimms was another neat ploy, but it was an act. Then Lew came gunnin' for whoever put him away, as you must have always known he would. You were ready for *that,* so you helped Mimms frame him *again.* An' *that's* when your boat started takin' on water.'

Scarlett was lying very still. He glared up

at Ansel, but now most of his fight had gone and he lapsed into silence. Cayne knew it was the truth he was hearing from the ranger, and his thoughts were wide-ranging and muddled. The man who'd pretended to be a supportive friend had double-crossed him, conspired to send him to jail on a false charge. Suddenly, ten years in the penitentiary felt like a long, meaningless lifetime.

'You snagged my interest after Cob Sholto broke into your ranch,' Ansel continued. Ever since the robbery, Ansel had felt there was something more, something about Scarlett's manner. 'When somebody's been through your house, fingered your chattels, you usually feel vulnerable an' resentful, not full o' piss an' wind,' he said. 'No one shrugs off two thousand dollars no matter how rich they are. There was somethin' *else* on your mind, somethin' that concerned you, but I didn't know *what* at the time.'

Scarlett shook his head. He wasn't disagreeing, simply accepting the inevitable.

'It was the gold. Doc kept your whiskey

company while you slipped off to check on it,' Ansel explained. 'How the hell would you have explained *that* away – gold bars bearing the new Wolf Hole stamp? It was one o' *them* that Sholto took with him. He took it from the stack you kept in the big desk under the foldin' cash.'

Scarlett almost smiled. 'Maybe, maybe not. You got to prove it, ranger,' he challenged.

'I can, an' I'm goin' to. Sholto's already talked. He only broke in to get somethin' to blackmail you with. He changed his mind at seein' the cash though, an' just couldn't resist one o' them bright golden blocks.'

'Who told him where the other stuff was?' Scarlett sniped.

'He took a long guess. Weren't too difficult for someone who knows every jack-rabbit an' gopher hole, like he does. Hah, an' that's where he dropped it. It accompanied young Josey Minch over the edge o' the arroyo. Where there's gold, the devil dwells, eh, Scarlett?'

Cayne made a sudden movement, as his thoughts became more focused.

'I ain't finished yet, Lew,' Ansel said, holding up a restraining hand. 'You might as well hear what else I got. When I realized Scarlett was workin' with Mimms, I sent Finney into town for him. I came up here, an' when Scarlett showed up, I *knew* it was *you* he was after. But I made a mistake in thinkin' he weren't suspectin' of anythin'. For that I'm sorry.'

'That's OK, but I can't think what it was he'd have told you. He said he'd think o' somethin'.'

Ansel nodded reflectively. 'You've been banged up for too long ... your mind's slowed,' he said. 'He'd have sworn it was whoever he'd been followin' who killed you. He'd have fired off his gun a few times for our sakes. By the time we'd have got here, your killer would've shown a clean pair o' heels.'

'Who would my killer have been then? Do you know? Framed someone else, would he?'

'Yeah, Simon Quinnel. He makes up a good story about the doctor, an' that conjures up a few unanswered questions.' Ansel looked down at Scarlett. 'How'm I doin', mister? Much wrong so far?'

Scarlett grunted, then shrugged, raised his shoulders high and tight. Then he relaxed into one fast-flowing lunge. His fist shot out at Ansel's knees, and the ranger faltered into a backwards stumble. At the same time, Scarlett was up and catching Cayne along the side of his face with another hard blow. They were the moves of desperation, and there was little else in Scarlett's reserve, just enough to fling himself out through the barn door to try and make a run for it. He stumbled a few steps, turned and glanced back.

But from quiet, gainful hiding, Remigo Correa was waiting. With regard to recent events, he knew most of what had happened, had already worked the rest out for himself. Like Ansel, he'd had doubts, but they were based more upon gut feeling. Right now, he took careful aim as Scarlett tried to make for where he'd tied in his horse. He tracked the man with the sights of his carbine, was fixing on bringing him down, when he noticed he was unarmed. He stepped into the open.

'This'll be the second time I got to draw a bead on you, mister,' he called out. 'An' if you're thinkin' I won't shoot an unarmed man, you're right. Not unless I find out you've harmed any o' my friends in that barn. Let's go find out.'

But Cayne and Ansel were both out through the door before Remigo had Scarlett at the barrel point of his carbine.

'We're all OK,' Ansel shouted. 'But he can hurt people with more'n bullets an' fists.'

'Let's get him hog-tied an' back to town,' Cayne said, holding his hand around his aching jaw. 'I want an end to all o' this.'

Ansel was of the same mind. 'Yeah, we all do,' he agreed. 'You know, someone's goin' to have to explain most o' this to young Josey, an' careful, too. Learnin' the truth about his guardian could be a bad influence on the way he feels about things. We can't have him totin' a jaundiced view o' life.' Then the ranger stabbed a short, distasteful glance at Scarlett. 'If you ever had a conscience, you got live the rest o' your life with it,' he said. 'That ain't my idea o' fun.'

And Ansel thought that Cayne was owed something. He hoped that Governor Degger would be generous and imaginative when it came to commendations for justice. Ten years was one hell of a wrong to put right. As yet, the rangers knew nothing of developments and actual events in Hackberry.

Above Song Creek's dried-out water course, Jack and Bryn Sholto gently held down the noses of their mules and waited silently. They'd been following Clarke Mimms and Morton Frome, were still a good distance from where the two men were lowering themselves over the lip of the arroyo.

'They must be above the cavern,' Jack said. 'If we're goin' to follow 'em, we'll be needin' our ropes.'

Ten minutes later, the boys were as quiet and effective as any desert hawk that swept down on its quarry. As they approached the darkly shadowed entrance to the cavern, they saw empty food tins lying in the arid creek.

'That's the second pile o' their rubbish we seen,' Bryn said.

'Yeah. Let's go in an' scare the billy hell out of 'em, then we can go take a look,' Jack whispered.

'This must be some sort o' camp. We'll wait until they got a lamp goin',' Bryn suggested, and they shared a grin in the moonlit dark.

For a few minutes the boys waited until they were sure the two men were deeper in the caves and busy with whatever it was had taken them down there. Then, they moved forward cautiously along the cut-back, trying to anticipate anything that came at them or made noise underfoot.

'What you shakin' for? You gettin' feared?' Bryn whispered, as they stood in the first of the water scoured hollows.

'Yeah, sort of,' Jack returned. 'They've lit somethin' ... must be next along. If we keep in the dark, we can get close. Don't make a sound.'

Now, just ahead of the boys, Mimms and Frome had pulled some empty bullion boxes across the floor of the cavern. Mimms was holding the stub end of a brush lamp, while Frome was tying the boxes into two stacked-up bundles.

'They ain't holdin' guns,' Bryn whispered again. 'Give 'em a scare to get things goin'.'

Jack nodded, fired both barrels of his scattergun up into the roof of the cavern. The blast was stupendous, and acrid cordite, mingled with all sorts of powdered dust. Bryn cursed and shouted, almost jumped forward to intercept Mimms and Frome.

As Jack reloaded the scattergun, Bryn stood among wreaths of smoke, smiled deviously as he levelled his pa's old pepperbox pistol at Frome.

'Reckon I know what you're thinkin',' he

said, his words echoing dully around the low-ceilinged chamber. 'That snot-nosed kid ain't hittin' anythin' with that piece o' junk he's carryin'. But what you should be thinkin' is this, when all six barrels go off at once.'

Frome looked to Mimms for a response, but there wasn't one.

'Life must be real cheap to these Sholtos.' Frome contemplated the effect of Bryn's pistol from less than fifteen feet. 'We broke away once, we can do it again. Meantime, an' if you still want to make it to Nogales, just do as they say,' he advised Mimms.

Jack snapped up the barrels of his gun. 'Watch out for Bryn, he's crazier'n me,' he threatened. 'Like as not, he'll shoot you with that pocket cannon just for the sheer hell of it. So both o' you get to the ground with your faces in the dirt. Keep real still, while I make tight, pretty bracelets out o' these ropes.'

After pushing the scattergun into the crook of his brother's left arm, Jack made a simple loop with each rope. Then he quickly slipped them around the ankles of both men and pulled tight. 'Now put your hands together, behind your back, an' don't forget Bryn ain't wanderin' off anywhere,' he said.

When the men's hands were securely tied, Jack slipped off the ankle bonds, took his gun back and told them to get to their feet.

'If we think you're makin' a break for it, we'll both shoot,' Bryn said.

'I guess you think you know what you're doin', kid,' Mimms spoke up. 'But how are you gettin' us out o' here, trussed up like this?'

'We're walkin' north,' Bryn answered. 'The ol' water-course goes underground, an' it looks like maybe there's another cut-back. We seen you already been there, an' we want to know why. It's no more'n a half-mile.'

Mimms nodded at the added misfortune. 'That's bad country. What happens then?' he said, concern cracking the edge of his voice.

'We come back. Then, usin' the ropes you used to get down here, we drag you both up top. We seen it done. But we might have to leave you,' Jack said, looking Frome up and down.

'Then it'll be *three* of us ridin' peaceable to Hackberry.' Bryn grinned. 'An' I just bet you had somewhere a lot further south in mind.'

19

Two days later, Governor Benson Degger was meeting with the three rangers. They were in the sheriff's office at Hackberry, and with them were Howard Teach, Simon Quinnel and Josiah Minch. Outside, the hard-packed dirt of the main street was shimmering in the heat of the noon sun.

'Things done by halves are never done right, eh, men?' Degger suggested.

Finney Proud shrugged, looked slightly tetchy. 'Well, *no one died,* did they, Governor?'

'No, and that's creditable. But there must have been a moment when you thought there'd be someone strippin' them vines from the old gallows,' Degger returned, with a wry smile.

Ansel was standing in the doorway for the

benefit of any through breeze. 'We can't even look forward to a worthwhile trial,' he observed.

The case which had moved so unpredictably away from Degger's original assignment for the rangers to investigate Clarke Mimms, was finished. Finished that was, other than the fact that after the fight, Mimms and Morton Frome had got away. In the general confusion outside of the hotel, they'd made a break for it *and* with most of the newly heisted bullion. But nearly a quarter of the missing gold remained and, as Ansel had guessed, it was in the deep drawer that Scarlett had hurriedly gone to check after Cob Sholto's robbery.

From the Hackberry jail, Scarlett, Wallace Egham and others from Mimms's outfit, had little to say. 'We ain't doin' your job for you. You got to prove all of it,' Scarlett had insisted.

Degger looked round the meeting he'd called. 'Well, the way it's turned out, we all got a little less business,' he said. 'It's a pity that Mimms an' his foreman got away a bit richer, but you ain't ever goin' to catch *all* the bad 'uns. If we did, all our jails would be overflowin'. We got Scarlett; we know who an' how it was worked, an' I ain't inclined to go over it with you all. As chief o' these rangers, Ansel, what've you got to say?'

'Sholto walked away, but I'll stand by that call. An' we can overlook Bleat's involvement. He's only got his past to answer to, not us. In any case, that would've been before he came here to join up with Mimms.'

Degger spoke up again. 'I appreciate what you an' the others had to say about Cayne,' he said with a nod towards Ansel. 'He'll be here soon, so I'd like to suggest–'

But the governor didn't get to make his suggestion. The doc interrupted him.

'Before we get to that, Governor, an' just so's we get everythin' clear, I got somethin' to say,' he said. Like a lot of professionals who moved among folk who weren't, Simon Quinnel often believed that whatever he had to say, took priority. 'It's just so we get everythin' clear, you understand?'

'We all understand that,' Degger said, as if he really did. 'But there's no need to worry. You ain't yet in line for the gibbet,' he added drolly.

'No, I know that,' Quinnel said, with an almost rueful smile. 'I was goin' to tell you that I thought maybe Mimms an' Scarlett were workin' together. There weren't one single thing to ever make us think they were enemies, like they'd have us believe.'

'This ain't relevant, or of much interest,' Finney stated, the heat and irritation obvious.

'But the next bit is,' Quinnel said. 'Doctorin' out here can get pretty borin'. Operatin' as a legal investigator seemed a bit less so. That's what I was doin' up at the Sholto cabin – snoopin' around, nothin' more. But what none o' you know is, is that it was me who wrote the governor about Howard.'

In quiet surprise, everyone looked from Quinnel to Teach to Degger. They all knew now that the doc wasn't a suspect, didn't figure in any recrimination. The story of the gun with the engraved butt that was planted in the coach, had come from Scarlett. It wasn't Quinnel, who'd made the mistake of reckoning that everybody knew about it. So what about this letter?

Degger looked tolerantly on the doc. 'I do recall gettin' a letter from someone who reckoned the sheriff was bein' blackmailed by Clarke Mimms,' he said. 'I got in-trays full o' that sort of emotional allegation. It's why they don't usually sign their name. Either that, or they don't know how to. But on *this* occasion, I did send some fellers to look into it.'

The governor's shrewd glance took in the rangers. 'I didn't tell any o' *you* because I didn't want any prejudice. I knew if there was anythin' hidden away, you'd find it. After that news o' rustlin' in Mexico, I wanted Mimms looked into with an open mind.'

The doc gave a relieved grin, but his eyes shifted unsurely to Teach. Remigo Correa was still wondering, still trying to estimate what was coming.

'I guess I'd better say somethin',' the sheriff said at last. 'An' folk have got to know sometime. Many years ago I made a mistake, an' ended up in jail for the price of it. I made good though, even got to be sheriff o' this town. But Mimms found out that some records hadn't been checked all that thoroughly. He knew that if they *were*, I'd be through. It was blackmail, o' course, but not for money. I couldn't have paid that. No, it was other stuff he wanted – information, deeds that I'd turn a blind eye to.'

'Are you sayin' you knew he framed Lew Cayne?' Ansel asked sharply, and on behalf of all of them.

'No. No, I swear I didn't know *that:* I always thought he was guilty. When I found out about young Josey, an' that Clarke was gettin' away with it, it all got a bit too much. That's when I told Finney. I told him that I'd got Dougal Bleat on side, an' that we'd help all we could, that I'd raise a posse, even.'

Finney was nodding in agreement. 'Yeah, that part of it's true enough,' he said.

Teach turned to Josey. 'When he wanted my keys, I never thought about what he'd be wantin' 'em for. Yeah, I knew about the dynamite, but I didn't think for one moment he'd be blown' up his own goddamn hotel with you in it. I swear to God I didn't, Josey.'

'Even bearin' that in mind, I think all in all, you're just about finished as a sheriff *here*,' the governor judged. 'There's always goin' to be a doubt over Mimms an' Frome escapin', despite the truth of it. But I'll get somethin' suitable for you across in Claypool. They'll be none the wiser, an' no one can pay more'n they're able.' Degger was a legislator, a politician who understood that having a man in a civil post wouldn't do him any harm. Lawful manoeuvrings were vital to his line of business.

The assembled men were now looking at each other. They were wondering where the next bit of enlightenment would come from, when they heard Lew Cayne shout. Ansel quickly took a step back onto the boardwalk and looked up the street, but it was a moment or two before he spoke. 'Christ, you better come an' take a look at this,' he said in astonishment.

20

Four men were riding down the main street. Out front, astride his saddle mule was Bryn Sholto. At the rear, and on a similar mount, was his brother Jack who carried a scattergun that was aimed unswervingly at the two men who rode between them. Clarke Mimms and Morton Frome were slumped in the saddle, hands roped behind their backs and ankles tied-in under their horses' bellies. They were hang-dog and unsteady, the horses roped in line, with Bryn loosely holding the lead end.

Townsfolk were jostling excitedly along the walkways to taunt and gawp. Ansel and his partners stared nonplussed, but Remigo Correa smiled knowingly, as though he'd been expecting something of the sort.

Frome made a sudden move to try to wrench his hands free. He jerked his arms from one side to another, but it was a futile act of defiance in the face of so many enthralled onlookers.

Nevertheless, Bryn twisted around and mouthed a menacing threat. Jack heeled his mule forward and slapped the barrel of the scattergun across Frome's right leg. His voice carried clearly to the sheriffs office.

'We told you once about playin' up. Try that again' an' you'll be ridin' straight on to the boneyard.'

A group of punchers moved forward, but Jack signalled for them to move away. 'We don't need your help. Didn't an' don't,' he shouted.

Frome's eyes blazed with anger, but his big, heavy body was well constrained. He was cursing long and low under his breath, but Mimms was keeping silent. Like Scarlett, two nights before, he seemed to understand that his big game was over.

Ansel stepped down into the street and Finney and Remigo followed. Within minutes they were outside the sheriff's office, had the prisoners' feet untied and pulled from their mounts.

'Get in there, the pair o' you,' Finney snapped. 'An' keep quiet or I'll go an' get Lew Cayne,' he warned.

'We took 'em at Song Creek, near the arroyo,' Jack said proudly, moving his mule towards his brother's. 'An' we found some gold bars. They were in another cave, maybe half a mile further on from where Josey Minch went over.'

Ansel drew a deep breath, puffed out his cheeks in surprised admiration. Unlike their pa, the Sholto boys had a streak of integrity running through them.

'How'd you make a gather on 'em?' he asked.

Bryn's expression hadn't changed from resolute. He held the reins in one hand, pulled the ageing pepperbox from a jacket pocket with the other. 'I used Pa's ol' Independence piece.'

'Yeah. A useful bit o' ordnance,' Ansel agreed.

For a few minutes, the men stood listening to the Sholtos' story.

'We knew where our pa kept it,' Bryn said, brandishing the distinctive firearm. 'He said they were real dangerous – said if you fired it off in a barn, you'd more'n likely kill everythin' in there. He bought it off a one-armed gunny in Tucson.'

Ansel grinned at the boy's wit. 'You saw 'em by the arroyo, did you?' he asked.

'Yeah, saw Frome first, an' we sort've tagged along. When we'd got 'em cornered in the cavern, we fired off just about every-thin' we had. It shook 'em up; we could see their mugs turnin' white in the dark,' Jack explained. 'They must've thought we were you rangers come to get 'em with a gang o' spooks.'

'Jack got 'em trussed up like a couple o' pot chickens,' Bryn said. 'Pa did tell us all them chores would come in handy one day.'

'Your pa said quite a lot in his quaint old way,' Ansel observed wryly. 'But you said you found some more gold?'

'Yeah, we did,' Jack said, 'further along. There was another long cut-back in the side o' the arroyo.'

'I guess it'll be safe enough until the morning,' Howard Teach said. 'There ain't anyone left out there likely to lift it.'

The Sholto boys' eyes crinkled up in their brown, wizened faces. They exchanged a cryptic, knowing look as a thought happened.

'He wouldn't,' Remigo said, and chuckled. 'But I'd know which horse to follow if he did.'

'Yeah. An' that just about winds up another excitin' day here in Hackberry,' Ansel said tiredly.

As the rangers stepped back to the office, Finney turned to the Sholto boys. 'Why'd you call that gun o' yours, an Independence piece?' he asked.

'I been waitin' for you to ask that,' Bryn said, with a rascally smile. 'Pa reckoned if it ever went off, it would be like the fourth o' July.'

And so it was, that the governor was able to talk with Lew Cayne. It was later, when Mimms and Frome had been reunited with Buck Scarlett. Together with Wallace Egham and half-a-dozen of Mimms's crew, they were securely behind bars in the sheriff's office.

'They're as packed up as mudfish,' Teach was saying. 'They've already had their first visitors, so they can stay that way for as long as it takes. But Remigo says there's a big rain comin' in, so we ought to get 'em out o' here, an' on the trail.'

'Who is it that's been to see 'em?' Degger enquired.

'Homer Chupp an' Juce Marble. They came to pay their respects. Offered to drive 'em all to Bullhead City for the trial. Then we talked about the county's policy on reward monies. They're sure deservin' of it. Lew had himself a word with Egham. I can't *imagine* what it was he could've said to him.'

'I more or less told him he weren't the

sharpest saw in his lumber yard,' Cayne responded. 'That now it was his turn for ten years. Thinkin' on it, probably *more.*'

'Hmm, that reminds me, Lew,' Benson Degger said. 'I ain't sayin' there's anythin' I can do to make up for all that time you spent in Yuma. There's nothin' can make up for *that.* But I *can* propose some sort o' restitution.'

Lew Cayne looked round the intent faces, at the three rangers, the doc, Teach and Josey Minch. 'Gimme a note sayin' I ain't goin' back,' he said.

'Even if I could, that don't seem like much to ask.'

'Ain't it? You ever done a jail stretch, Governor?'

'No, can't say I have.'

'If you *had,* you'd know that that was one hell of an ask.'

'I'm talkin' of compensation,' Degger pointed out. 'A sum large enough to buy you a few valley sections o' pasture.'

'Oh right, yeah. Well wouldn't that be

somethin'? Maybe I could employ. Nothin' lowly o' course. I'd be lookin' for four, maybe five top hands.'

'I'd be interested,' Josey said. 'An' how about the Sholto boys? Don't seem like any of us got much in the way o' family.'

'Yeah, why not?' Cayne's grey eyes brightened, and he agreed with a hopeful smile. 'But we'd have to run 'em through a dippin' vat. We wouldn't want 'em ploughed in as manure.'

Degger gave a kindly smile. 'Stand 'em out in the rain. There's goin' to be plenty of it here soon enough.'

21

'It weren't so long ago, Homer was tellin' me he was stickin' to his post until we got right to where we're goin',' Juce Marble, said. 'Well, I'm makin' this ride for *him*. Neither of us was paid for not gettin' there.'

'Well, this time you got a couple o' rangers an' a sheriff for company, an' we ain't jumpin' ship until we get to that place we're goin' to,' Ansel Agnes affirmed.

'You might not be sayin' that in an hour's time,' Juce rumbled on. 'I reckon you'll be wishin' to join them downstairs.'

From their corner seats inside the Concord stage, Howard Teach cradled a scattergun, and Remigo Correa his carbine. They were the armed escort for Wallace Egham, Morton Frome, Buck Scarlett and

Clarke Mimms. They were being taken to the cells at Bullhead City to await trial, safe, until the circuit judge arrived at the beginning of the following month.

Governor Degger had secured employment for Teach as one of the city's deputy marshals. In Hackberry, Finney Proud had agreed to stay on as a law officer until a new sheriff and deputy could be appointed.

'Homer would've lied about his shoulder,' Juce said. 'But it's still givin' him grief. He just didn't want to give up this opportunity. He'd'a wanted to see that barrelload o' scum sittin' there miserable an' defeated. Mind you, gettin' a reward for it's cheered him up some.'

'That's good to hear, Juce. But meantime, we don't know whether there's any o' their kith or kin out here lyin' for us.'

Juce pulled the palm of his hand down across his ragged moustache. 'If they got any sense, they'll be gettin' 'emselves hunkered down. Either way, I'll just call for these horses to quicken their pace a tad,' he suggested drily.

Twenty miles out of Hackberry, the coach was negotiating a long dipping trail bend when the rain started. Ansel checked with Remigo, and they pulled alongside a stand of spruce to pull on their ponchos. As the horses ran further west, the sky grew steadily darker and the rain increased. It wasn't long before they heard the creek water start its low, ominous growl.

With lightning flickering and thunder rolling in from behind them, Ansel tugged down the brim of his hat. 'Wouldn't want to be back in that arroyo when *this* storm hits,' he said. 'I hope Finney got the gold brought in. They could get 'emselves washed clear to Bullhead ahead of us.'

'I'm not too certain I want to be *here*, when it hits,' Juce hooted grimly. 'We got Needles Bridge comin' up.'

The storm water was now rising, highly coloured but not yet wild enough to under-cut the banks. At the crossing, Ansel got down and walked ahead. He could see the trestle timbers glistening wet in the meagre light, waved for Juce to bring the coach on as he walked forward. They'd make it across, but he could feel the bridge shudder as the current whirled and pummelled the braces. Where they'd swing out from the higher ground was still another twenty miles on. But from there, the road would sweep through more open country, along the flats and on to Bullhead City.

Moments ahead of the waves of thunder, blinding bolts speared the sky and Juce called reassurances to the team. 'Jesus, if we ain't into the mother of all storms,' he shrieked above the noise. 'Could be ol' Homer had this one tagged. An' right now he's somewhere grinnin' up at the roof over his head.'

Ansel watched in awe as dazzling spectres of fire danced on the horizon ahead of them, the horses' eyes bulged and their ears flattened as they ran in dread. Then, the rain changed direction and came in low, full in the face, as if the creek itself was being pitched up at them.

Juce was going to tell Ansel that if it wasn't for the lightning they wouldn't be able to see the road ahead. But he thought better of it, settled into the terror of their flight and grinned wickedly at the thought of the prisoners' frame of mind.

Sparks streamed from the brake shoes as the coach made a bend in the road. Juce drew his great bull whip and, as the coach lurched on, he cracked the long rawhide lash sharply over the leader's ears. He held the reins taut and sawed at the bits, kept the horses steady until he felt their response. They raced the nightmare for more miles, searing flashes lighting the dark creek water ahead of them. Water surged up to the hocks of the bays, rain lashing against them as they ran.

After ten miles or so, Juce knew they had a good chance of making the Bullhead City fork, but as they got closer, there was a sound that worried him; something that ran against the roaring of the creek. He soon realized that it was the sound of water rushing down from the peaks. It was racing into the bend ahead of them, straight across the road and into the creek.

The water grew relentlessly deeper and swifter. The team sensed immediate danger, fought the rising cross-flow run. Juce realized that he should have cut the team loose back at the bridge, let everybody make their way to the relative shelter of higher ground. But he cursed and cracked out the lash again.

Ansel jabbed his arm. 'The arroyo,' he yelled, above the roar of the water.

Juce shook his head clear to clear his thoughts, realized the horses and coach couldn't make it. The wheels were turning slow in water that was almost axle-deep.

Ansel shook his head, pointed down to the inside of the coach. 'We got to get 'em out o' there ... all of 'em. Peach an' Remigo can keep 'em covered.'

Juce snorted with disgust 'Up here you ain't chief, *I* am. I was under their guns, don't forget, so they ain't gettin' out for more'n a piss. An' that's from me *an'* Homer, even if we *all* drown.'

22

Juce Marble whooped, cheered on the horses, cracked the bull whip out into the menacing darkness. Up ahead he could just make out the road where it widened. He knew it was where an arroyo turned away from the main creek, about a mile east, and this side of the Bullhead City turn off.

When the mines were working full out, riders who knew the country had used the dry watercourse as a short cut to the main wagon road. Freighters would haul over to take a break and let the stage through. But now, Juce Marble's coach team was slipping and floundering in its harness as he eased the horses forward. He yelled frantic encouragement at their gruelling progress, dragged savagely at the bit of the near-side leader as the team turned into the mouth of the arroyo.

The road water was now being displaced by the arroyo's flooding, and Juce was considering the coach's toughness and stability. But if any vehicle could make it, he knew the old Concord could. Frequently, they dropped to a walk, the lead horses picking their way along the bank side like a span of pack mules. They had to stop once where the road narrowed, and Juce had to walk the leaders around a rocky outfall. But then he upped the pace, under the now slackening rain, let them feel the let-up of his stress through the reins.

A half-hour later they ran from the arroyo, swung onto the open road that led to Bullhead City. The horses sensed the trail's end and ran willingly towards their stabling with its feed and shelter.

'Some goddamn drive for a land lubber,' Ansel said, just about the only words the two men had exchanged since before the arroyo turn-off.

Juce took a deep breath, then gave a thin

smile. 'We got that gold *half* the goddamn way here. I wonder why the Wolf Hole bosses didn't think to let us finish the job?'

'Oh, they'd have thought of it, Juce,' Ansel said. 'Probably reckoned that with a gang o' stage robbers actually on board, it weren't such a good shipment. Too much of a temptation, armed guard or not.'

Juce thought for a moment, then grinned. 'Yeah, maybe. So let's have a song,' he offered. 'I'm reminded of a few lines that Homer was particularly keen on.'

'Well, long's it ain't too jubilant. We're not there yet,' Ansel warned, with a wry smile.

Juce coughed, found a low musical note from the back of his throat.

I shot me a coon an' a waterhole rat,
Knifed a rattler an' a mean polecat,
Ate 'em all with a fish out o' Jango Creek;
Should feel a lot better, come Sunday next
week.

'Hah, an' that was one o' Homer Chupp's

favourites, was it?' Ansel laughed. 'Just as well there's only a few o' them lines.'

'Never once got me to finish a whole song,' Juce chortled.

As they approached the outskirts of the town, the storm abated and holes of inky blue appeared through the dark overcast sky. Then the moon sailed free, lit the sprawl of the city's main buildings ahead of them.

'I guess it ain't the way you'd got it figured, Juce, but you've made it here, after all,' Ansel said. 'What will you be spendin' your reward money on?'

Juce spread his arms expansively wide. 'If it don't move, I'll buy it. They got stores here with so much stuff, they even got floors stacked on top of each other.'

Ansel gave an appreciative grin. 'Yeah, so I hear. An' I got a shoppin' list from the Sholtos to deal with,' he said.

'Hah, that's rich,' Juce hooted. 'Comin' from a family that's never had more'n a pot to piss in.'

'Well they sure got one now. Old Cob

Sholto left behind a couple o' thousand dollars when he rode off. Arguably it's part o' Buck Scarlett's assets, but he won't have need of it where he's headed, an' I certainly ain't goin' to argue the legitimacy o' the case.'

Juce eased the team into a relaxed canter. 'With all our business, it's just as well we're goin' back with a half-empty coach,' he replied.

The publishers hope that this book has given you enjoyable reading. Large Print Books are especially designed to be as easy to see and hold as possible. If you wish a complete list of our books please ask at your local library or write directly to:

Dales Large Print Books
Magna House, Long Preston,
Skipton, North Yorkshire.
BD23 4ND

1	2	3	4	5	6	7	8	9	10
11	12	13	14	15	16	17	18	19	20
21	22	23	24	25	26	27	28	29	30
31	32	33	34	35	36	37	38	39	40
41	42	43	44	45	46	47	48	49	50
51	52	53	54	55	56	57	58	59	60
61	62	63	64	65	66	67	68	69	70
71	72	73	74	75	76	77	78	79	80
81	82	83	84	85	86	87	88	89	90
91	92	93	94	95	96	97	98	99	100
101	102	103	104	105	106	107	108	109	110
111	112	113	114	115	116	117	118	119	120
121	122	123	124	125	126	127	128	129	130
131	132	133	134	135	136	137	138	139	140
141	142	143	144	145	146	147	148	149	150
151	152	153	154	155	156	157	158	159	160
161	162	163	164	165	166	167	168	169	170
171	172	173	174	175	176	177	178	179	180
181	182	183	184	185	186	187	188	189	190
191	192	193	194	195	196	197	198	199	200
201	202	203	204	205	206	207	208	209	210
211	212	213	214	215	216	217	218	219	220
221	222	223	224	225	226	227	228	229	230
231	232	233	234	235	236	237	238	239	240
241	242	243	244	245	246	247	248	249	250
251	252	253	254	255	256	257	258	259	260
261	262	263	264	265	266	267	268	269	270
271	272	273	274	275	276	277	278	279	280
281	282	283	284	285	286	287	288	289	290
291	292	293	294	295	296	297	298	299	300
301	302	303	304	305	306	307	308	309	310
311	312	313	314	315	316	317	318	319	320
321	322	323	324	325	326	327	328	329	330
331	332	333	334	335	336	337	338	339	340
341	342	343	344	345	346	347	348	349	350
351	352	353	354	355	356	357	358	359	360
361	362	363	364	365	366	367	368	369	370
371	372	373	374	375	376	377	378	379	380
381	382	383	384	385	386	387	388	389	390
391	392	393	394	395	396	397	398	399	400